I0561124

PHANTOMS ARE FOREVER

CONFESSIONS OF A CLOSET MEDIUM BOOK 9

NYX HALLIWELL

BEACH PATH PUBLISHING, LLC

CPhantoms Are Forever

©2024 Nyx Halliwell

ISBN: 978-1-964028-11-8

Cover Art by Fanderclai Design www.fanderclai.com

Formatting by Beach Path Publishing, LLC

ONE

W hen I came up with the idea to hold a town swap meet, I didn't consider how many ghosts would show up.

On a bright spring morning in May, I move through the growing number of vendors, my clipboard gripped tightly in one hand and a pen in the other. Like a determined bee flitting from flower to flower, I check off each booth with a sense of accomplishment as those who've registered arrange their wares.

Thornhollow's Magnolia Market blooms before my eyes on the high school football field, evolving from an empty canvas into a vibrant kaleidoscope of colors and buzzing potential.

"Morning, Gordon," I call to a burly man in overalls hauling a crate of handmade soaps. I give him a map and guide him to his spot in the crafts and services section. "You're two stalls down from Kit."

"Thanks, Ava!" he replies, his arms effortlessly lifting the crate as if it weighs no more than feathers.

A heavenly scent floats through the air. "Be sure to save me two bars of lavender-eucalyptus," I say, ignoring the phantom spirit of an Irish Setter following at his heels. "And two oatmeal for Logan."

"You got it!"

At least the ghost clinging to him is canine. Across the way, Larissa Loomis' grandmother hovers near as Larissa lines up buckets of cut flowers she's grown in her green-house. The grandmother isn't an earthbound spirit so much as a guardian angel, but I see Larissa batting at her shoulder and ear as if a fly is buzzing around her head. Grandma is needling her about not having enough yellow tulips—her favorite—or lilacs.

Next to Larissa is Pete Younkers and his two teenage daughters, placing fresh produce and eggs on the three tables they've set up in U. With them is the girls' mother's spirit. She's earthbound, and it's no surprise why—she refuses to cross to the afterlife, fearing she won't see her girls grow up.

I know all of this because I'm a ghost whisperer. A medium. I see and hear the dead.

I am also the president of Thornhollow's Chamber of Commerce, and in January, when I came up with the idea to have a spring swap meet complete with a farmers market and food trucks, I also made a resolution to myself—no more ghosts.

Having this ability has nearly gotten me killed several times and put a strain on my relationships with friends and family. Although I've helped bring peace to certain folks by assisting their loved ones in finding closure and moving on, I took a hard look at what doing so has nearly cost me after my wedding last October. Any person with an ounce of sense can see the risks far outweigh the benefits.

At least, that's what I keep telling myself.

"Tell them," Olivia Younkers calls to me. She wrings her non-corporeal hands. "Tell them I love them. Tell them I'm here!"

If only it were that simple. As a successful business-woman who runs a wedding gown boutique along with my Aunt Willa's event-planning business, I have other responsi-bilities. Many people in town knew my aunt had the gift. In these parts, many fear such abilities or, at the very least, ignore them, chalking it up to things better left alone.

Those who are more open to the possibility still feel uncomfortable if you walk up out of the blue and tell them their loved one has a message. The spirit may believe it would be a welcome piece of news, but I've discovered it often does more harm than good.

Returning my attention to my clipboard, I keep walking. If I have an opportunity at some point during this weekend, I'll pull Pete aside and see if he's receptive to receiving a message from his dead wife. However, if I'm going to keep my pact with myself, I need to ignore her.

The sod on the football field is damp with dew, coating my shoes as I walk from one end zone to the other. The tasks loom like a mountain waiting to be conquered, but I'm pleased to see my mountain coming to life before my eyes.

My intern, a teenager named Lia, trudges up to me, yawning. Her hair is in pigtails, and her sleepy eyes are half closed behind her round Coke bottle glasses. The forecast is perfect—temperatures in the 80s and no rain on the radar—but she's wearing a jacket and long pants. Her backpack is chartreuse and covered with pins about ghosts and aliens. "Where do you want me?" she asks.

"Good morning to you, too. You look like you need a cup of coffee from Queenie." I've placed the three food vendors in the center of the field, back to back, forming a divider between the farmers market and the flea market. "I don't think she's open yet—we don't start till eight—but I'm sure if you knock on the back door, she'll get you some breakfast. It's on me."

Queenie is my mother's best friend and runs a successful restaurant in town. One of her big dreams has always been to have a food truck, and she purchased an existing one online from a guy in Atlanta. She's only had it two weeks and is remodeling the inside, but the little silver Airstream already came equipped with a generator, running water, and a counter for her to serve customers. She's added a refrigerator, several appliances, and a grill top.

Lia's shoulders slump, and she glances toward the high school. "I had to study for a math test last night," she tells me. As part of her work-study, I get her for three hours this morning before she has to return to classes this afternoon. Since the football field and track are not in use this time of year, it was the perfect venue for Magnolia Market's inaugural kick-off. Her unfocused gaze returns to mine. "I hate algebra."

"I did, too." I put an arm around her shoulder and turn her toward the spot at the gate where I've set up a welcome table. "Your station is there. You'll find a clipboard just like this"—I tap mine with my pen—"with a list of our vendors and flea market sellers. There's also a stack of maps for the public to show where each booth is located and what they're selling. If a vendor comes to you, send them to me and I'll help them find their designated stall. Most are already here, but a few stragglers are to be expected."

Since February's initial sign-up, I've been emailing and calling those who paid a fee to join the meet. However, people are people, and there are those who never opened a single message.

An ethereal figure is searching the grounds. She dashes behind a sign Logan painted indicating the furniture and vintage rows when she realizes I've spotted her. Her hair is gray and thin, and she's wearing a sheer nightgown. A *very* sheer nightgown.

Thank goodness I'm the only one who can see her. I may have to ask my spirit guide, Persephone, to wipe that picture from my mind.

Lia follows my line of sight. "What is it?"

"Nothing." Sadie Haversham has arrived and is flagging me down. I wave and call, "Your spot is on the end of Estate Row." Yes, I've divided every section of the field like city streets and named them. I put a checkmark next to her on my list. "Number seventeen."

She gives a thumbs-up and tugs a child's red wagon full of her grandmother's possessions behind her.

Estate Row—definitely staying away from that section. Spirits not only anchor themselves to loved ones and their former homes, but they also piggyback on their precious possessions. The flea market has multiple estate and antiques sellers today.

"Are there ghosts here?" Lia asks, suddenly more perky.

"Not a one." I don't feel guilty about fibbing. She's part of a select circle who knows what I am and finds it exciting. She and a small group of friends consider themselves ghost hunters and have a club. "I better get back to work."

"You always say that where the living gather, so do the dead."

"Since when do you listen to what I say?"

She ogles the field. Knowing her, she'll be texting her club members before I can check the next thing off my list. "Sage and Kit agree."

Since Lia works for me, I agreed to allow my witchy friend, Sage, and my psychic friend, Kit, to train her in handling and protecting herself around spirits. But she's among the reasons I'm sticking to my resolution not to engage any unless absolutely necessary. At my wedding reception, a ghost shot me and could've hurt a lot of others. I've had nightmares ever since, and Lia has starred in many of them.

"Today, we're focused on the living," I say, scanning my list, "and you have a table to get to. Under it are boxes of t-shirts and tote bags with our Magnolia Market logo on them. The shirts are twenty dollars and the totes are ten. See if you can sell a few, okay? It's good advertising."

"Yeah, yeah." She rolls her eyes and heads for the food trucks. "See ya."

"Ask Logan to help you with your algebra," I call after her.

She raises a hand in acknowledgment and keeps going. I

notice how she keeps checking around in hopes she'll spot a ghost.

I scan the half of the field where the flea market will take place. Logan, my handsome husband, is somewhere in the crowd of sellers, ensuring each stays within their allotted space. He's used temporary spray paint to outline each stall, and while this is my first time walking the field, it probably feels like a type of homecoming for him. He was a quarterback when we were in school.

"Avalon!" Mama strides across the damp lawn. She waves, looking freshly showered and dressed in a smart suit and heels. Her graying curls are pinned close to her head, and her makeup is perfect. "I'm here!"

Yes, she is. When Thornhollow's mayor, Dixie Fantome, makes an entrance—even on a high school football field at seven in the morning—no one can miss her.

She envelopes me in an Aqua Net and Chanel No. 5 cloud, along with a fierce hug. "My, this is *impressive.*" This is said as if she had serious doubts I could pull off such an event. "I don't know why I didn't think of it myself."

"We did it together," I say, and it's true. "If I hadn't had your support, I'm not sure the council would have given us the green light."

She waves a hand dismissively. "It's like digging a pond and hoping for ducks—they don't always act on the good sense God gave them."

Mama has an expression for everything. Many of them don't actually make sense, and yet, being Southern, I understand them all. In this case, I assume she means they aren't proficient at planning or understanding how to set successful goals. "Guess it's a good thing they have you."

This earns me a smile, along with an elbow nudge. "Don't be cheeky."

I grin. "Never."

She scans me from head to toe, lingering on my jeans and running shoes. In her world, every public appearance should be met in your Sunday best. "What can I help with?"

"Everything is under control."

"There must be something."

Another thing to add to my list—keeping my well-meaning but sometimes overbearing mother occupied. "Can you track down Logan and make sure he has enough tables for the flea market sellers? They were supposed to supply their own, but you know how folks are."

Mama rises on her tip-toes, scanning over the melee. "I just saw him..."

"And you better stop by Queenie's truck—she's really nervous about her soft opening today."

She pats my arm. "I'll keep her calm."

She strides off to find Logan first. Steering Mama's helpfulness is akin to redirecting a river—necessary yet challenging. Sighing softly, I turn back to face the increasingly growing crowd. Time is already getting away from me—I only have forty minutes before we open the gates to the public.

"All right, checklist, let's dance," I murmur to myself.

More farmers arrive, and so does Kit. "Did you bring it?" she asks, keeping pace with me as I direct several of our service vendors to their designated sections.

My stomach lurches, and I glance around to see if anyone is listening. "Yes, but..."

Her long skirt is tie-dyed yellow and violet and swings

around her ankles as she spins in a circle, searching for the bowling ball bag I carry the item in. "Where is it? Did you already put it in my booth?"

She's a private detective who recently moved to town moonlighting as a psychic. The thing is, she really *is* psychic and does more business giving tarot readings and making predictions than she can outing cheating spouses or proving insurance fraud. "It's still in my car." I fiddle with my pen. "I'm having second thoughts about loaning it out."

Her brows shoot up under the matching tie-dyed turban she's wrapped around her head for effect. The Great Madam X is as serious about her outfits as Mama is. "You don't trust me?"

"Of course I do. It's just that Aunt Willow's crystal ball is... Well, it's an heirloom. It's not like I use it, but I feel connected to her through it."

She squeezed my arm. "I promise to guard it with my life." She's been wanting to get her hands on it for months. "Divination tools are created to be used, Ava. Not stored in a bowling ball bag in your attic."

I bite my lower lip. "I know. It's just..."

"Just what? Have you had a vision?"

I chuckle. "Heavens, no. I'm not like you."

She gives me a tolerant smile. "You're more like me than you'll admit."

My spirit guide, who fancies herself a guardian angel, appears out of nowhere. "Stick to your guns, Ava," Persephone says. "That crystal ball has the ability to attract unwanted attention."

Kit and I both freeze—while I can see and hear Persephone, my friend can only hear her. She should count her blessings. Today, Persephone's outfit is a red fire engine jumpsuit with a gaudy rhinestone belt and orange high heels. Her chandelier earrings are lime green, and she has a sky-blue scarf circling her neck. The clash of colors is nearly blinding.

"What do you mean?" I ask, blinking through the glare.

In true Persephone fashion, she vanishes without answering.

She hasn't been talking to me since I gave up ghost whispering, so this is her way of vexing me. It's working. "I hate when she does that," I mutter to Kit.

Kit handles this stuff better than I do. "Drop a dire prediction bomb on you?" She gives me a reassuring smile. "She's a master at it."

"That she is."

"No worries. We can skip using the ball. I better finish setting up."

I'm genuinely nervous about handing over the heirloom, which is literally the size of a bowling ball. Aunt Willa claimed her husband—my uncle, who was an avid bowler—always teased her, saying he was going to use her divination tool to help improve his score.

But Kit is right. If Aunt Willa were here, she would share the thing without a second's hesitation. That's how she was—generous and kind.

Thinking of her, I dig out my car keys from my pocket. "It's in the trunk," I tell Kit, handing them to her. "Be careful."

Her eyes light up, and she squeezes my arm. "Thank you. I promise to treat it with care."

As she hurries to retrieve it, I glance heavenward. "I hope I'm doing the right thing, Aunt Willa."

A breeze lifts the ends of my hair, and I'm about to take that as a sign from her when the ghost in the sheer nightgown appears before me.

"Stop wasting time and help me," she demands and knocks the clipboard right out of my hand.

TWO

I check to see if anyone's watching and snatch up the clipboard. "Go away," I say through gritted teeth.

"This is all your fault." Her face is lined with wrinkles, and the finger she points at me is misshapen with arthritis. "How could you let her sell my stuff? Stop her!"

I stare at the clipboard and scribble on the corner of a page, trying to look busy as I mutter, "I don't know what you're talking about or who *she* is. You need to leave."

"I was told you could help me."

I flick my gaze to her. "Who told you that?"

The gnarled finger aims like an arrow across the field. "Her."

Persephone idles next to Queenie's food truck, giving me a wave. Before I can lift a brow, she disappears.

"She lied. I don't do that anymore." Especially not for rude ghosts.

I start toward Craft Row. We have knitters, woodworkers, jewelry makers, and a lady in her 80s who takes discarded quilts and chenille bedspreads and turns them into animal pillows. They're adorable, and even though I don't need one, I zero in on her display, trying to keep my pulse from racing. Maybe I'll buy a few as gifts.

The old woman materializes again, making me jump. "You're going the wrong way. Sadie is in the flea market, idiot!"

I divert my eyes from her angry face and nearly naked body. Spirits often appear to me wearing the clothes they died in. This gal most likely passed in her sleep.

I blow out a breath, trying to figure out how to get rid of her. "What's your name?"

"Edith Haversham. Don't you know me? Your Mama and I go way back."

That doesn't exactly narrow it down. My mother knows everyone in the county. Always has. When I was a child and we would go anywhere, the trip would take twice as long as it should because a dozen people would stop and talk to her. I once asked her if she knew everybody in the whole world because that's how it seemed to me. "Sorry, the name isn't familiar, and neither are you." No one is watching us, but that won't last for long if I stand here appearing to talk to thin air. I generate enough gossip in this town without adding to it. "You should stop worrying about Sadie and move into the light."

"Ava?"

I jump again, but this time, Sage has snuck up on me. I grab my chest. "Geez, don't do that."

She hands me a muffin, examining the space I was talking to. The scent of lemon and blueberries teases my nose. "Ghost trouble?"

I stick the pen on the clipboard and rip off the top of the muffin. "What's new?"

"Do you need help?"

I bite into the treat and chew with vigor, taking out my frustration on the food. "Can you get rid of my guardian angel?"

"We've discussed this. Even if I could, that would be a bad idea. What has she done now?"

"Dropped a prediction bomb on me and sent an earthbound spirit my way, trying to force me to break my resolution."

Sage gives a sigh. We've talked about this subject as well. "Denying your gift isn't the solution."

I swallow, not even tasting the muffin. "Well, I can't say using my gift has done me any favors."

She watches me consume the rest. "I get it. No good deed goes unpunished, right? But I can tell you from experience that the more you fight against it, the worse things will get. And, while I know you don't want to hear this, it's not about the Universe doing you a favor in exchange for you doing one for the greater good."

"Isn't that how it's supposed to work? What goes around comes around? The law of three, or whatever you witches call it?"

"This isn't you talking. You're kind and generous, and you've always done what you could for everyone, both living and dead. I know what happened at your wedding scared you, but swearing off ghosts isn't the answer."

"Stop offering sage advice, Sage," I tease with a half-hearted smile. It's time to change the subject. "Is Biz coming to see you?"

He's totally in love with her, and I think she is with him, but she tries to hide it. The edges of her mouth quirk as she attempts to hide her grin. I'm not sure if she's in denial of her feelings for him because of a previous heart-break or if she just doesn't know how to handle a relation-ship. She never talks about past boyfriends, and I'm not sure she's ever had a serious one. "He's already texted twice to see if I need anything, and we're not even open yet. By the way, I appreciate you letting me set up a booth. I know this is more for amateurs who don't have a brick-and-mortar store."

I finish the treat and actually taste the lovely blend of flavors. "Thank you for providing me with breakfast. I didn't have a chance to get anything before I left the house. And just so you know, the rules the Chamber and City Council agreed on state that any store owner who's been in business less than a year qualified." Her shop, Tea Leaves, is located across from my place and offers food and drink along with tea leaf readings. "It's beneficial for both the store owner and our town to advertise our small businesses."

"Is your ghost gone now?"

"Yes." I'm glad, too, but I suspect she'll be back. "She's a strong one. She knocked the clipboard out of my hands." I'm gripping it tightly, my anxiety returning at the thought. Most spirits can't move objects unless they have an enormous amount of energy. That energy comes from strong emotions, such as anger, or from draining it off the living they latch onto. "Her name is Edith, and she's upset about her grand-daughter, Sadie, being here."

"Is Sadie a vendor?"

I brush crumbs from my hands and flip a page over on

the clipboard. "A seller on the flea market side. She's in Estate Row."

Sage gives me a knowing look. "She's selling some of her grandmother's estate, and grandma is still attached to her things."

"Looks like it." Two craft vendors pass us, chatting, on their way to the food trucks. We exchange greetings, and they continue on, while Sage and I wait for them to get out of earshot. "I'm staying as far away from that row as I can get. There is sure to be more than Edith's ghost over there."

"Ava," she starts.

I hold up a hand. "Look, I've helped over a dozen spirits cross to the afterlife since I moved to Thornhollow. If that was all I had to do, I would embrace my gift with open arms. But something bad happens every time I start mucking around with the spirit world. I can't keep taking that risk."

She gives a sigh, and her focus goes over my shoulder. "Let's discuss this more later."

I glance back to see Logan approaching. He's wearing a baseball shirt with three-quarter-length blue sleeves. He's obviously been wiping his hands on the white front, his hair tousled, and his jeans muddy. "Hey there," he says to me in his deep baritone, dropping a kiss on my head before he gives Sage a nod. "Are y'all set up, Sage? Need any help?"

"I'm good. Thanks. If you need a pick-me-up, I've got muffins."

"I'll be over shortly."

She gives a wave and leaves.

He moves closer, grabbing me by the arms and pulling me against him. "You're the prettiest girl here."

"Why, Mr. Cross, haven't we discussed not calling me a girl?"

He nuzzles my neck. "It's meant with the most loving intention, but if you're offended, allow me to make it up to you later."

I chuckle and swat at his arm. "Back up, *boy*. You're all dirty."

"Now you *do* sound like a girl," he teases with a smile that makes my heart skip. His wheat-colored hair glistens in the sun, and he's already got a hint of a tan.

We share the old Victorian mansion my aunt left me, running The Wedding Chapel Event Planning Services and his attorney business out of it. "Go get a T-shirt from Lia and tell her to put it on my tab. Did Mama find you? Is everyone set up in the flea market?"

He brushes at the dirt on his stomach, but it's a hopeless cause. "The last seller just arrived, but he has it under control thanks to Dixie's help. Everyone else is good to go. What do you want me to do next? Give you a shoulder massage? Bring you some coffee?"

"I could use both, but I'm going with the coffee for now. We don't want to scandalize the Magnolia Market before it's even open."

He checks his watch. "Speaking of."

In a panic, I grab his arm to check it myself. "Oh, no." I've been so distracted I've lost track of time. It's two minutes to eight!

I scan through my list once more, but the few things that haven't been checked off will have to wait. I peek at the front gate and see there's already a line. People are pulling into the parking lot in a steady stream. "Gotta go," I tell him. Thanks for all your help."

He gives me a quick kiss. "At your service, Mrs. Fantome-Cross."

Together, we race to the closed gate. He gets a shirt from Lia and ducks behind the bleachers to change. A few people on the other side of the barrier wave and call 'good morning' to me. The school bell rings, and I take a deep breath, smiling at the growing crowd. *Please, let this be a success.*

As the bell dies away, I raise my voice. "Welcome to Thornhollow's first Magnolia Market!"

Just as I open the gate, Edith appears in my peripheral vision. "You can't let them in," she shrieks.

And then she slams into me, knocking me to the ground this time.

THREE

I hit the ground hard enough that my breath whooshes out of my mouth. Folks pile in, and Lia jumps to her feet. "Ava!"

A man in a trench coat and hat helps me to my feet. "Are you all right, ma'am?"

I collect myself and brush dirt off my jeans. "I'm fine, thanks."

He has thick gray sideburns and deep wrinkles around his eyes. The corners crinkle as he studies me. "You look like a truck hit you."

A skinny one in a sheer nightgown, but still. "Guess I lost my balance, that's all." I pick up my clipboard for the second time and grab a map from the stack on the table. Lia also asks if I'm okay, and I give her a nod. "The football field is filled with great things to buy," I tell the man. "Would you like a map?"

"No!" Edith cries. She floats past us, holding out her hands as if to strangle me with her gnarled fingers. "Don't help him! Don't let anyone buy my things. They need to stay in my family!"

He studies the paper intently, a frown on his face. "Yes, I see that."

"Is there something in particular you're looking for?"

He folds the map and shoves it into the coat's pocket. "I think I see what I want." He tips the edge of his hat to me. "Have a good day."

As people stream by, some of them nod and greet me. "Good morning," I call to everyone, exchanging my clipboard for a stack of maps. I hand them out as fast as I can, tickled that so many are here already. "Welcome, welcome. We have produce, crafts, food trucks, and a flea market. Don't forget to buy a tote bag, and be sure to come back tomorrow."

Logan arrives and joins Lia behind the table. He takes over selling T-shirts and tote bags while she answers questions. People flood the field, going in all directions, and as soon as I'm out of maps, I pause for a moment to look for Edith. She's gone, probably off haunting her granddaughter and anyone who buys the last of her possessions.

At the first break in the action, I make a note to recruit more volunteers for the next day. Lia guzzles a drink. "Why did you fall down?"

Logan looks up from digging in a box. "You fell? What happened?"

The shirt he's wearing is too small. "You need an extra-large," I tell him while admiring how the tight fabric defines his chest and biceps.

"That's what I'm searching for." He tosses a folded one back in the box. "You don't seem to have any XLs."

I scurry around the table and paw through the box

myself. "There should be twenty of them. Where did they go?"

Logan grabs my arm, stopping my search. "When did you fall?"

I wave it off. "I stumbled on a piece of rock when I was opening the gate. No biggie."

He and Lia exchange a look. "It was a ghost, wasn't it?" she asks.

"Don't be silly." I grab another box from under the table and open the top. "Those shirts have to be here."

And then it dawns on me and I straighten. "I know where they are." I reach into my pocket for my keys, but they're not there. "They're in my trunk. Kit has my keys."

"I'll get them," Lia offers.

Logan shakes his head. "I'll get the box. You two have your hands full."

He stalks across the field toward Kit's booth, and Lia returns to her seat as a group of women enter through the gate. I greet them, and she hands out maps.

"Where is that psychic?" one of them asks. She's wearing a ball cap and sunglasses and peers around me toward the end zone.

I use my pen to point out Kit's location on the map. "She has a large sign across the front table. You can't miss her."

The woman nods and leaves the other three, who are busy checking out the T-shirts.

While Lia helps them find the size each needs, Baylor Davis, our librarian and vice president of the Chamber, rushes up to me. "I got here as soon as I could. What can I help with?"

Her cheeks are flushed, and her brown curls are held

back by a headband with honeybees and expressions like *Bee kind* and *Bee yourself* on it. She's wearing a light sweater with a honeybee brooch that matches and a yellow pleated skirt.

Mama will approve.

We hug briefly, and I point toward the beginning of the farmers' section. "Check in with each booth owner and see if they need anything. Start there and make your way around the entire field."

"Good thing I wore my walking shoes," she says. Her southern accent is soft and calming. "Looks like we're off to a great start. It was a brilliant idea, Ava." She points to the ladies completing their purchases. "Should I wear one of those?"

"And cover up that pretty outfit? No way." I dig out a badge from my pack hanging on the fence and hand it to her. It's on a lanyard and reads, "Coordinator."

She puts it on and pats it. Someone calls to us with a question if we have any quilters, and she grabs a map. "I'll take care of them. See you in a bit."

That's one of the best things about her—she jumps right in and helps out. I'm lucky to have her as my vice president, and the town is equally fortunate to have her as the librarian.

Two teenagers file in, one a tall, lanky boy with his hands in his pockets and the second a short, pudgy girl with braids like Lia's. She gives a squeal as her customers file off. "You made it."

The boy glances at me and then away. The girl hugs her before they dance, complete with hand gestures that football players who've scored touchdowns could emulate. "Mr. Cravits gave us twenty minutes," the girl says.

"Travis, Wrenlee, this is Ava. Ava, these are my friends."

"Nice to meet you," I say.

"We got out of study hall," Wrenlee tells me.

"Torture hall is more like it," Travis adds, digging the toe of his sneaker into the ground.

"Well, have a look around and enjoy yourselves." I pat Lia's shoulder. "I can handle the table. You go with your friends."

"You're the best." The two girls take off running across the field while Travis trudges slowly behind them.

The rest of the morning flies by. Lia has to attend classes after lunch, so I grab a sandwich and chips from Queenie to eat while I handle the welcome table. People trickle in and out, and many of those leaving haul treasures with them. Bigger items, such as repurposed and antique furniture that are to be picked up later, receive an orange *Sold* tag and are lined up along the bleacher side of the fence. The buyer must show me their receipt before I hail Logan to help them carry and load the item into their vehicle.

Baylor's shift at the library begins at three. She carries two full totes as she prepares to leave. "See you tomorrow," she says.

"Did you get anything good?" I ask.

"Macramé hanging for my living room, some antique jewelry, and a few gifts. James Starling had a bunch of vintage classics. I had him put those aside for the library. I'll get them tomorrow." She pauses at the table. "Sadie Haversham has a unique collection of herbal folklore and...*recipe* books. Very unusual. Not sure they're right for our patrons, but maybe you should have a look at them? I wouldn't want them to fall into the wrong hands, if you know what I mean."

I lower my voice and make sure no one's around. "Witchcraft?"

She shrugs. "Maybe? Not my area of expertise."

Mine either. "I'll check into it."

Setting a sign on the table to let new arrivals know I'll be back soon and to help themselves to the maps, I tuck the cashbox under my arm and head to Queenie's truck. I slip in through the side door. "How's business?"

She's wiping down the counter and stacking several clear containers with prepackaged salads to the side. Her dark, kinky hair is high on her head, and perspiration dots her smooth forehead. "Better than I anticipated, but Lordy, I need air conditioning."

"I'm glad you're selling well. I knew the truck would be a hit."

"You're the one with the golden touch around here. Where'd your mama run off to?"

"I haven't seen her; she's probably talking to each and every person here. You know how she is. Say, will you hold this for me?" I ask, showing her the box.

"You look like you're on the way to meet the Grim Reaper," she says. She waves the towel at a shelf under her register. "Leave it there and tell me what's put that frown on your face."

"Nothing. Sorry, I'm all up in my head about this market. I thought Brax would stop by." It's true and seems like an excellent way to redirect the conversation. "And Rhys."

"Honey child, they'll be here. They're busy fellows. Their B&B is packed for the weekend, and The Toad has plumbing problems."

Brax is my best friend—we grew up together. He and his

partner run several ventures in town, including the bed and breakfast next to my place and The Thorny Toad, where Kit does psychic readings. I tuck the box behind a pile of napkins. "I'll keep an eye out for them."

She sneaks a piece of candy from her display. It's a chocolate-covered pecan concoction that resembles a turtle. "This will make you feel better," she says with a wink.

I chew on that while I walk to Sage's. She's placing three packages of loose tea in a bag and adding her business card to it. "There you go," she says, handing it to her customer.

The woman thanks her and moves on to Kit's booth. Sage pockets the bills. "How's it going?" she asks.

"Great. Can you take a break?"

"Now?"

Several folks are examining her offerings. "Never mind. I'll see if Kit's free."

Kit has an older lady behind her table, reading her palm. I don't want to disturb her.

Guess I'm on my own.

As I cross by the food trucks again, hearing a trickle of guitars from Taco Bandito's speakers and catching the scent of seasoned meat, I murmur, "Persephone. I'm going to Estate Row, and I know Edith is there. If you want me to help her, you need to help *me*."

I slow my steps, casting a glance around. No spirit guide. *Fine. I'll handle this myself.*

The moment I enter Vintage Row, right before Estate Row, Carl Anderson assails me. "Ava," he says, coming out from behind his tables lined with gaudy jewelry. I'm surprised my guardian angel isn't here picking out a piece for her collection. "An expensive necklace of mine is missing. It was right here." He points to a standing peg board with hooks holding various old pieces. "It had real emeralds in it."

"Missing? Is it possible it fell off, or you simply misplaced it?"

He shakes his head. "The pendant alone is worth a hundred dollars. I had it appraised after I bought it at an estate sale. I can show you the papers."

"And you're sure you didn't sell it?"

He gives me a look that suggests I'm a moron. "It is one of my prize pieces! Of course, I would know if I sold it."

I hadn't anticipated theft—another thing to add to my checklist for next year. "I'm so sorry, Carl. I can't believe someone would steal from you. Do you have any idea who it might've been?"

"I've been swamped. I should've brought my brother to keep an eye on my inventory while helping customers. I've never had this happen before, though, at any of the other sales I've attended."

His tone suggests it is somehow my fault. "You do this often?"

"I buy and sell all over the state, and I've never once had someone steal from me."

"I am sorry, and I'll see what I can do. If you want to file a claim, I can call the police for you."

"Why *wouldn't* I? That piece is worth money."

"Was it insured?"

He frowns. "No, but...don't you see? That's why I have to get it back. Otherwise, I'm out that money."

I take out my cell as he doesn't finish. I make a note to contact my father, as well as the police station. "I'll notify the

Thornhollow PD, but you'll have to speak to an officer directly."

"Well, I don't have time to do that. You'll have to take care of it for me."

I know how these things work because my father was once part of the department. However, instead of arguing with Carl, I walk away. As I pass Furniture Row, I text Daddy. *There's been a theft at the market. What should I do?*

Of what? he responds. *A head of lettuce?* He adds a smiley emoji.

A piece of expensive jewelry.

Any idea who stole it?

Would I be texting you if I knew?

Touché. The three bubbles of a follow-up response appear, so I wait. *Want me to come down? I'm free this afternoon.*

That would be great.

Another set of bubbles. *Anything for you, sweetie. I'll let Landon know there's some suspicious activity going on.*

Detective Jones and I don't get along, and the last thing I want is him snooping around my big event. *Can we leave him out of it for now? I'd rather you investigate first.*

Sure. See you in a few.

I feel better about the whole thing. Daddy will know what to do, and if he and I can't recover the necklace, I'll notify the police department and let them handle it from there.

Unfortunately, my plan to keep Detective Jones out of my hair crumbles before my eyes when I see him in full uniform, taking notes on his trusty blue notepad while speaking to Lorna Cummings. They're in front of her set of three tables of assorted garage sale knickknacks. "It was made from ash and had a Celtic symbol on the top."

"And you last saw it where?" he asks.

"Right here." She points to the table on her right. "Next to the crystal skull."

"What's going on?" I ask.

"Someone stole a puzzle box from me," Lorna says, wringing her hands. "It was here not twenty minutes ago. I went to the bathroom—Steve was keeping an eye on things for me—and when I got back, it was gone. Leo Kingsley from Story Cove is coming to look at it. He said it might be more valuable than I thought."

Jones makes a note. "Who's Leo Kingsley?"

"He deals in antiquities," I tell him. "Mostly vintage and out-of-print books, but also other collectibles and heirloom items. Sage knows him."

"I didn't see a thing," Steve, Lorna's neighbor, chimes in. He's a big fellow wearing a baseball hat and red boots. His drawl is pronounced. "I had a bunch of customers right after she left. Guess I should've kept a closer eye on her stuff."

"I want to report a crime!" We all turn to see Sadie Haversham marching toward us. Inwardly, I groan. "One of my grandmama's prized recipe books is missing!"

"See?" Edith appears behind her, giving me a condescending glare. "You should have made her take all my stuff home! She never should have brought it here."

A crowd descends on us, drawn in by the commotion. A few are vendors, and others are shoppers. Detective Jones scans the group. "Did any of you see anyone suspicious?"

They shake their heads and murmur among themselves.

One lady speaks up. "I looked at that box earlier but couldn't figure out how to open it."

"That's why it's called a puzzle box," Lorna snaps.

"I would've bought it if you could've shown me how it worked," the woman snaps back.

"Okay, okay." I hold up my hands and step between them. "Who else was looking at the box?" I ask Lorna. "Did anyone seem particularly interested in it?"

She chews on her bottom lip, seeming to concentrate, but shakes her head.

A short, balding man across from me says, "There were a couple of high school kids hanging around, pawing everything."

Another murmur runs through the crowd, and Steve nods adamantly. "They were at my booth, too. Two different groups of them. And a teacher came by on his lunch."

Jones makes another note. "Any of them acting suspicious? Did they appear overly interested in any of your..." He scans the items on the tables, struggling to find a non-offensive word for what he considers junk. "Things?"

Carl Anderson joins us, pushing through the crowd. "I want to make a claim. My emerald necklace is missing. Those kids were at my tables, too. I bet they stole it!"

It's distressing how the mob mentality sets in so quickly. One minute, everybody is curious; the next, they're all glaring at the school and nodding at the thought of a teenage thief.

"Ava!" Kit jogs up, out of breath. "There you are." She takes a second to suck in several lungfuls of air.

"What is it?" I clasp her arm to support her as she bends at the waist. "Are you all right?"

"I don't know what happened." Her eyes are filled with remorse. Her headband is askew. "I'm so sorry."

My gut sinks. "Sorry about what?"

She straightens and licks her lips. "I swear, I was keeping a close eye on it."

My grip tightens. "Close eye on...?"

"It's gone," she says, her face pinching. "I messed up, Ava. Someone took your Aunt Willa's crystal ball."

FOUR

My stomach sinks to the ground. "What? Are you sure?"

Detective Jones flips to a clean page. "A crystal ball?"

My heart raps hard in my chest. How could this happen? "My Aunt Willa's. Kit borrowed it for her readings today."

"It's huge." She uses her hands to show him the diameter. "It's not like someone could slip it into their pocket and walk off with it."

"Is the bag still there?" I ask.

"Under my table where I put it."

"Anything else from your booth missing?" Jones asks.

She shakes her head. "I was discussing sensitive stuff with a client, so I walked her behind my table for more privacy. There were a lot of people filing by. When I returned, it was gone." Her sad eyes land on me again. "Persephone was right, wasn't she? Her prediction?"

"Don't tell her that," I mutter. "She's already insufferable."

Jones narrows his eyes. "Who is this Persephone?"

I wave him off. "Trust me, she had nothing to do with the crystal ball's disappearance." At least, she better not have. If she's doing this to prove a point... "Whoever stole it must be the same person who took the other items."

He gives me a stern look, not appreciating the fact I won't answer him about Persephone's identity. He wouldn't like it if I did. "That would be my guess. Anybody have a reason to believe they were taken by more than one thief?"

"I'm telling you," Carl says, "it's those kids."

The crowd issues a chorus of agreement. Jones raises his hands to quiet them. "Y'all go back to your business. I'll look into this and speak to each impacted vendor one-on-one. For those of you here shopping, if you saw someone eyeballing the items in question or anyone suspicious, line up under the goal post, and I'll be with you shortly."

As people file away, some point at the school while others type on their phones, spreading the word.

Jones put his hands on his hips and scowls. "I'll take your statement last, Ava. In the meantime, get your clipboard and check with all the other vendors to see if they're missing anything. If they are, get a description of the item, who was interested in it, and if the vendor has any suspects in mind. Report back to me when you're done."

While I feel responsible for this mishap, I want to start searching for the crystal ball. His gruff manner, on top of my already full stress load, sets me off. "I don't work for you." Maybe Kit or Sage can use their psychic abilities to figure out who took the ball and where it is. "Get one of your officers here to help you."

"You're in charge of this gig, right? Therefore, you take partial responsibility for what happened to these folks."

He doesn't need to remind me, but I'm torn. I didn't have any security in place, and even if I had, I'm not sure they would have caught our thief. Or thieves. The missing crystal ball feels even more important now, a keepsake I can never get back if this all goes wrong.

I take out my phone and text Lia. *Trouble at the market. Things have gone missing, and there are high school students who may be suspect. Come see me as soon as you can.*

"Why didn't you ask for descriptions of the students?" I ask.

"I'm getting to that," he growls. "Don't be thinking you can tell me how to do my job, Fantome."

He does that on purpose—leaves off the Cross in my hyphenated last name—anything to annoy me. Usually, I correct him, but today my fuse is too short and I refuse to let him get the best of me. "I wouldn't have to if you knew what you were doing."

Kit "eeps" and pulls me away. "Why don't you come with me?" She gives Jones a smile. "We'll find Logan and he'll help Ava question everyone."

If Jones could set me on fire, he probably would, but he gives her a polite nod. "If you uncover any further...particulars, let me know."

We both know what he's insinuating. He claims not to believe in psychics, but if we have 'insider information,' he'll use us to crack his case.

She puts an arm through mine. "Of course. Anything I can do to be of help."

Once we're out of earshot, I lean toward her. "As an investigator, you're three times better than he is."

"Only three? Honey, he's not all that bad, but I'm ten times the investigator he is, and it's not because I'm psychic. He has a narrow view of the world and must follow the rules. I don't."

"Good. I don't care whether you use your psychic skills or good old-fashioned detective work, we have to find that crystal ball. And more importantly, the other things that were stolen. This could ruin the market before it's even finished its first weekend."

She squeezes my arm. "No one's going to ruin the market. We'll retrieve those items. Biz is watching my booth. I better get back. Can you handle your assignment on your own?"

"I'll do my best."

Over the next thirty minutes, Daddy arrives, bringing Brax and Rhys with him. Logan and Biz join us, and I fill everyone in on the details. We divide the field according to the yard markers, and each takes a section.

At the fifty-yard line, I check with my food vendors. None of them report anything suspicious. Queenie tells me she'll close early and help question the flea market sellers.

Around three, Lia shows up, stomping toward me. "You think my friends did this?"

My automatic reaction is to say 'no.' However, I can't rule anyone out. "I'm sure they had nothing to do with the thefts, but several groups of students were in the vicinity of the missing items, according to their owners. We have to consider every angle."

"I can't believe it."

"Can you talk to them for me? Do some detective work

together. I know they weren't involved, but they may have seen someone acting suspicious or heard other kids talking about the stolen items."

"What I mean is, I can't believe *you*. You actually considered the idea that Wrenlee and Travis did this. What's next? Are you going to have Jones take me down to the station and interrogate me?"

I'm exhausted, anxious, and doing my best to ignore the ghosts trailing after me, each demanding I do something for them. Edith, Larissa Loomis' grandmother, and Olivia Younkers. "Don't be ridiculous. I don't suspect you, and I don't suspect your friends, either. But we have to nip this in the bud, Lia. Many people around here believe high school students did it, and Wrenlee and Travis were here and fall into that category, along with you. I know you visited Sage and Kit. Who else?"

Her look tells me I have fallen off the pedestal she keeps me on. "The soap guy and a couple of the women selling jewelry in the craft section. Wrenlee loves rings."

"You didn't go over to the flea market? There are several tables in the vintage section, as well as the general flea market, selling jewelry."

Lia screws up her nose. "Not that old stuff. She likes modern rings. The gal who runs Simply Charmed has a laser cutter. She puts all kinds of cool symbols and pictures on silver bands."

I've seen them and thought about buying one or two myself. "And you're sure Wrenlee and Travis didn't return without you and circulate through the other half of the market? With the old stuff," I add.

"Maybe at lunch? We have different lunch periods. But even if they did, they would never steal anything."

"I know, but check with them to see if they saw or heard any other students talking about the market or showing off an emerald necklace, a puzzle box, or a crystal ball."

Her mouth falls open. "Willa's crystal ball?"

"Yep." A necklace and a puzzle box could be easily hidden in a purse or tote bag, but not that beast of a divination tool. "I can't imagine how they snuck it out of here, but then again, I couldn't watch the gate the whole time."

"I should've skipped classes today."

I put an arm around her shoulders and we start walking toward the flea market. "This is not your fault, and classes are important. Did you ask Logan about tutoring you with your algebra?"

"Our first lesson is tonight at seven."

I give her a squeeze. "Do you need a ride to my house?"

"Nah. Travis has his license now and, don't tell his mom, but he's got a side hustle hauling some of us around. Three dollars a ride."

Oh, Lord. "I don't think that's a safe idea." And I'm pretty sure it's against the law without an adult in the car with them. "Save your money. One of us will come and get you."

She brightens. "Can I stay the night? It only makes sense since I'm going to be here all day tomorrow."

I can't say no to her. "You're always welcome to stay, but be sure it's okay with your mom."

She throws her arms around my waist and hugs me. Then she takes out her phone. "The ghost hunters are on it. I'll text Travis and Wrenlee, and they can help us with the investigation, even though it's not ghost-related." Her fingers fly over the keyboard. "I'll catch up to you."

I interview two of the Furniture Row booth owners and then cross paths with Detective Jones coming from Vintage Row.

"I've taken care of the rest. What do you have?" he demands.

"Nothing. No one else is missing anything." I tell him about my team. "We're reconvening at the gate at closing time."

"I'll get your statement then."

"There's not much to tell. It's a crystal ball. I gave it to Kit. She had it at her booth. Now it's gone. What else do you need to know?"

His cell rings, and he takes the call, dismissing me without a backward glance as he stalks away.

After the last customer leaves and we are all gathered at the gate, I consider what I'm going to do about the situation overnight. Most of the vendors have packed up their valuables and left. My overnight security consists of Hank Newsom, a retired police officer who's on the city council. For his services, the chamber is donating billboard space for his wife's hair salon.

It seemed like a bargain at the time, but I hadn't anticipated the fact I'd be faced with the current situation. I'm sure Hank is sufficient for what we need, but the field is a big place, and the fences are easy to climb. With all the booths and food trucks, there are plenty of places for kids, or those up to no good, to hide when he makes his rounds or even if he takes a break on the bleachers. He's sixty-five, and I have no doubt he'll need one or two, or maybe even succumb to a nap.

None of us have come up with other missing items—which is a relief—but neither do we have any leads. Several booth owners expressed concern to me before they left, and I did my best to reassure them that I will have volunteers in place tomorrow, keeping an eye on their merchandise. This seems to ease their worries, but three of them said they won't be back.

I can't blame them.

Mama arrives, flustered at the news, and after Jones joins us, she gets into it with him over his approach to the whole thing. "I've had a dozen calls from parents this afternoon about you accusing their kids of stealing."

"I haven't pointed the finger at anyone," he says.

"The general consensus in town is that you suspect a high school student."

He doesn't miss a beat. "Maybe more than one."

"This is why they're calling me! Leta is rallying them."

He shrugs, not the least bit worried about the school board president raising her parental army. "Not my concern. Finding the crook—or crooks—is."

I admire Jones' courage—or maybe his stupidity—in the face of Dixie Fantome's outrage. Daddy cuts off Mama's next tirade. "Do you have everything you need from us, Landon?" He asks his former partner.

Jones gives me a look. "For now."

Daddy pats my shoulder. "I'll watch the grounds tonight with Hank."

"Maybe I should stay, too," I say.

Logan shakes his head. "You're barely keeping yourself upright. Go home. I'll hang out."

Brax, towering over the rest of us, rubs the stubble on his chin. "Go home, now, Ava. I've got this."

Daddy nods in agreement. "Take her home, Logan."

Mama embraces me. "Make her rest."

My friends and family are incredible. "I appreciate all of you."

"I'm spending the night," Lia says, bouncing on her toes. "Not here." She points at the turf. "With Ava and Logan. But I've got to go home and get some clothes."

"We'll take you," I tell her, slipping my hand into my husband's. "We can pick up dinner on the way."

"We'll be over after I smudge myself," Sage says, cocking a thumb at herself and Biz. "I'll bring my pendulum."

She uses it along with a map to locate people and things. I see Jones screw up his nose, catching on. He pretends to study his notes, avoiding our gazes.

"Good." I turn to Kit. "You come, too. Let's see if we can get a hit on the ball."

"Are you feeding me?" she asks.

"We'll pick up extra," Logan says.

She smiles. "I'm at your disposal."

With that, we disband.

FIVE

I have incredible friends. Biz insists he'll take Lia home to grab an overnight bag while Sage packs up and smudges herself.

By the time I finish the final cleanup and preparations for Saturday and Logan and I arrive home, we discover Kit, Mama, and Queenie waiting for us.

My husband orders pizzas while the women gather drinks. I check the messages Rosie left for me after holding down the fort while I was away. I hold out three orange slips to Mama. "You're not the only one receiving calls from concerned parents."

She snatches them from my hand and stuffs them in her purse. "Don't you worry about it. I'll take care of them."

While we wait for the others and our dinner, Queenie makes me walk her through the entire day from start to finish, asking questions about the stolen items and the vendors who were selling them. "What do they have in common?" she asks.

Logan and I are on the couch with Kit. My cats, Arthur and Lancelot, are curled up on either side of me. Mama and Queenie are in chairs we brought from the kitchen, and Logan has poured them glasses of wine.

I shrug. "Besides the fact they were all stolen?"

She toys with her glass. "I mean, is there a link between them that you haven't thought about yet?"

"We have a necklace, a puzzle box, a crystal ball, and some cookbooks. Each was stolen from a different vendor in a different location. The only thing I can see that they have in common is the timing. They were all taken this afternoon, approximately around the same time."

"Is there anything we—the victims—have in common?" Kit asks. "A common enemy, perhaps?"

Last year, she was psychically attacked, and it left scars she still isn't entirely over.

Queenie waggles a finger at her as if she's thinking that as well. "Or maybe the items originated from the same place."

"That can't be," I say. "Kit got the crystal ball from me, remember?"

"Right." She sips her wine, tapping her fingernails on the glass.

"Why did you dig out that old thing from Willa's belongings anyway?" Mama asks.

She was always uncomfortable with her sister's abilities —and that discomfort extends to mine, as well. She accepts that I am a medium, but that doesn't mean she likes it. I suspect she has the gift, too, and because of her fear of it, has stifled it but good.

"It's my fault," Kit explains. "When Ava told me about it,

I knew I had to see it. It's the biggest one I've ever encountered, and I wanted to use it."

"Size matters," Queenie says with a wink.

"Hush now," Mama says, giving her a playful tap. "Why aren't you satisfied with the one you have?"

Kit quirks her lips to one side. "It's like you noticing a problem in the community. You need to fix it, right? It bugs you until you take charge and do something about it."

She is speaking my mother's language. "Yes, that's true. "

"Well, for me, after I saw it the first time and felt how much energy it had, I couldn't stop thinking about it. It could do so much good in the world and give people answers that they are yearning for. You and I have different ways of helping folks, but that's what we do, and we're not content to sit on our hands if someone needs us."

Mama nods and raises her glass to Kit. "The world needs more people like us."

An orange marmalade cat strolls through the living room, giving me a pointed look. Tabby is my many times great-grandmother in feline form. She was a powerful witch back in Scotland, where she was born, and if I'm not mistaken, her magical abilities have only grown through the years. Trailing behind her is her husband and my ghostly grandfather, Samuel. The two of them founded our town several hundred years ago. "We've heard there's been some hubbub," he says to me as he hovers near the fireplace.

Kit stiffens, and I know she's heard him, but only I can see him. I am saved from trying to explain to him and Tabby what's happened when Sage, Biz, and Lia come through the front door.

Lia hangs her backpack on the hook next to it. "Did we miss anything?"

Logan gets up to help Biz and Sage get drinks for themselves, and I recruit Lia to help me drag in the office chairs to add to our gathering. While we do that, I ask about her friends. "Did you text them?"

"Yes, and like I told you, they had nothing to do with it and didn't see anybody else we know hanging around the booths."

It doesn't rule anyone out, really. Travis and Wrenlee were only there for a short time by my calculations.

She wheels in Rosie's chair while I bring in mine. "I'm sorry I had to ask you to do that. As you know, when we investigate cases, sometimes we have to do uncomfortable things."

Logan and the others return, and he hands Lia her favorite carbonated water. Then he refills wine glasses.

Mama thanks him and sighs dramatically. "I hate to say it, but maybe it *was* a student who nicked the items. They certainly had means and opportunity."

Lia stands defiantly. "I'm sorry, Miss Dixie, but it's unfair that everyone wants to blame the teenagers."

"The thefts could be completely unconnected," Logan says. "We could have multiple thieves, and we have to be careful that we don't focus on any one suspect while the real one is right under our noses."

My husband, always pragmatic and logical. He would've made a good cop, but he's an even better lawyer. He looks at every problem from multiple angles.

Sage withdraws a velvet bag and a rolled-up map from her tote. "I can't tell you who stole the items, but maybe we can see where they are right now. Do you have anything that was close to or touched the crystal ball?"

Kit jumps up, disturbing Lancelot. He gives a disgruntled cry, and I stroke his back. "I've got the bowling ball bag in my car."

"That would be perfect," Sage says.

A minute later, we gather around the kitchen table where she has rolled out the map of our town. She removes a copper pendulum from the velvet bag, holding it in her hand for a long moment with her eyes shut. When she opens them, she places it inside the bowling ball bag.

The old leather smells musty. As we watch, she holds her hands over the top of the opening and begins to silently move her lips. Could be a spell or a prayer, the two often very much the same.

Tabby hops up on the end of the counter to watch, Samuel hovering nearby. Biz peeks in from the doorway. The room grows hotter by the moment, probably from all the body heat since it's relatively small, but also from the magic that's rising.

Lia's eyes are big behind her glasses, Kit has closed hers. I assume she's working to amplify Sage's magic. Mama downs her wine like my cats inhale their food every morning.

Sage's lips continue to move, and I feel a tingling heat rush up my spine. When she finishes, she removes the pendulum and dangles it over the map.

At first, the copper doesn't oscillate. We are all quiet, holding our breath, and I say my own little prayer. *Please let this work.*

Ever so slowly, it begins moving. At first, it goes side to side, then begins a counterclockwise motion.

Sage frowns, grabs it with her free hand to stop it, then tries again.

"What's wrong?" I ask.

"Shhh." She closes her eyes, a tiny crease forming on her forehead. "Everyone focus on the map with the intent of finding the lost items."

All of us, except Mama, step closer, doing as instructed. My mother disappears out to the back deck, and my cats follow.

We've disturbed Moxley, Logan's basset hound, from his sleep. I hear his thick nails coming down the stairs from the second floor. I place my hands on the table, my attention on the map, ignoring his snorting and sneezing as he ambles into the room. He goes to Logan first, who gives him a quick pat, and then he comes to me and licks my bare ankle.

I jump. Then I pet his head quickly and return to focusing.

The pendulum does the same routine. First, it swings east and west, then rotates counterclockwise.

"Shoot," Kit says.

"What does it mean?" I ask.

"You can't find the crystal ball," Sage says. "I'm sorry."

Logan taps the edge of the map. "Can't you keep trying?"

"Won't do any good." Sage returns the pendulum to her bag. "Either someone has it under a protection ward, or it isn't in town."

My stomach sinks. What if our thief has taken off across the state?

"Can we get a bigger map? One that covers more territory?" Queenie suggests.

Biz squeezes Sage's shoulder as she rolls up hers. "Divination like this becomes unreliable the broader the area to be searched. I'm not an expert douser, but I suspect we need a different approach."

"What if I try to get a hit?" Kit asks.

"I thought you already did," I say.

She shrugs. "Can't hurt to try again."

"You should ask a ghost for help," Lia offers. "We could do a seance!"

I send her a chastising glare. The last time she was part of one, held around this very table, she couldn't sleep for a month afterward. "No seances." At least not until I'm desperate. "Go for it," I tell Kit.

She nods and grabs the bowling ball bag, taking it into the living room and plunking herself in a chair. We all tag along to watch. Even my grandparents are totally invested, Samuel staring at the ugly bag and Tabby circling Kit's ankles.

"All right, crystal ball," Kit says, closing her eyes. "Talk to me."

She's silent for a long few minutes. Again, we collectively hold our breaths. I see something change in her face, and when she finally speaks, her voice is monotone. "I see a boy's hands. Dirty fingernails. He's caressing the crystal, then sticking his hands in his pockets. Touching it again. Hefting it off its stand, and..."

Lia has gone rigid. "And what?"

Kit blinks open her eyes. "Oh, lord."

"Did you see who it was?" I ask, feeling desperate. Something about her description nags at my memory. Dirty fingernails. Hands in pockets. "Anything besides his hands?"

Kit nods, giving Lia an apologetic glance. "I saw his face.

Maybe we should talk in private," Kit suggests to me, casting a purposeful look at Lia.

"No," my young intern says, paling. "You're wrong."

Kit gives a sad shake of her head. "I'm not."

"He wouldn't do it," Lia insists.

My heart sinks.

Logan glances between all of us. "Who? Who stole it?"

Silence hangs for a heartbeat, Kit and I waiting for Lia to come to terms with it. Finally, she does.

"Travis," she says, voice strangled with emotion. "My friend took the crystal ball."

SIX

The following morning, we're awake early again. Logan lines up coffee mugs and fills them. Sage brings over muffins. Kit shares a pint of strawberries she bought from Pete Younkers and his daughters.

I wanted to confront Travis last night, but he doesn't seem like much of a flight risk. Lia was so upset that we spent an hour after our pizza trying to reassure her. I also fielded more calls from parents and vendors who were upset about the situation.

Today, I will find a way to question the kid and get my crystal ball back.

Rosie is handling an afternoon wedding with the assistance of our part-time employee, Jenn. Tessy Borage and Brian Judson are having a small affair at the church. They've been married before—to each other. After five years of being divorced, they've decided to try again.

I'm hustling everyone out the door when I hear Lia say, "It's about time you showed up."

Filing out to the wide porch, we discover Travis leaping up from one of the rocking chairs. "Come on. It's Saturday. It's the only day I get to sleep in."

She pokes him in the chest, nearly knocking him back into the seat. "Tell her you didn't do it."

He looks sheepishly at me, sliding his hands into his pockets, but his voice comes firm. "I didn't steal anything."

Kit and I exchange a glimpse. Could she be wrong? I hope so, but I've never known her visions not to contain at least a grain of the truth.

"I saw you, Travis." She uses her calm, *you can't fool me* voice. "I saw you lift it from the stand on my table."

He shuffles from foot to foot, eyes darting about but not landing on any of us. "I wanted to get an answer to my question. I looked at it, sure, but then..."

I motion for him to resume his seat and for the others to back off. Sage draws Lia to the other side of the doorway, giving us space. Logan leans against the railing, sipping his coffee like this kind of thing happens daily. Kit takes the other rocking chair.

"Start from the beginning," I say. "Why were you at Kit's booth?"

"We went to see her," he says. "Me, Wrenlee, and Lia."

"Lia introduced them to me," Kit says with a nod.

"She told us Kit was the real deal, and I had a question. It was personal, so I went back a while later to ask it. Thing is, I didn't have enough money to pay her."

"Wrenlee wasn't with you?" I ask.

He takes his hands out of his pockets as he eases back down. His hands aren't still, though. A thumb taps on the arm of the chair while the other hand picks at his jeans. "Nah. I didn't want her to know."

"Know what?" I ask.

He glances Lia's way and then at the porch. "I'd rather not say."

Oh, boy. Lia takes a step toward him. "You better tell us. This is serious, Travis. If you nicked that ball—"

He starts to come out of the chair and then thinks better of it when Logan clears his throat before he continues the questioning. "You had your hands on the ball and took it off the holder, right? Then what?"

"Then I saw something weird," he chokes out.

Tabby makes an appearance, coming up the steps and winding her way past me to glance at the boy. I hear the gargoyles who sit at the top of the stairs muttering: *He's guilty*, the first one says. The second joins in. *Look at that face.*

Yes, these inanimate objects have been infused with magic. They have a telepathic connection to me when they choose to use it. The door knocker adds his two cents. *He's certainly not telling the truth.*

I'm not sure if my aunt enchanted them or if my grand-mother, who is currently circling my ankles while she listens, did. Either way, I find it's best to ignore them. "Weird in what manner?" I ask.

He rocks. "Just so you know, I don't believe in this stuff."

Kit snorts, and Sage rolls her eyes.

"But you wanted to ask Kit a question, and because you didn't have the money to pay her, you thought you would gaze into a crystal ball?" I verify.

A flush starts at the base of his neck and works its way up

to his cheeks as he rocks faster. "Look, I'm sorry I touched the ball, okay? But I didn't steal it, that's all I came to tell you."

When his gaze darts to Lia again, I consider making her leave. Whatever his question was, it obviously has something to do with her. "I'm afraid that's not good enough," I tell him. "I have no one who can confirm your story, so if you're not going to be honest with me, I'm going to talk to your parents."

That does the trick, as I suspected it might. He jumps to his feet and paces to the end of the porch, then returns. Raking a hand through his hair, he lowers his voice. "All I wanted to know was if she would say yes if I asked her to the dance. I was going to take the ball for a minute, that's all, then bring it back. I swear. But when I looked into it, I saw my sister. My *dead* sister."

"I'm sorry. I didn't know you had lost someone close to you."

He hugs himself. "She was ten years older than me. She drowned when I was seven."

Kit narrows her eyes. "She must've had a message for you."

He stares at the wood planks beneath him. "She sure did. She told me to put the ball back."

"Still don't believe in this stuff?" I ask, hiding a smile.

He flicks a quick glance at me, then down to Tabby, who now sits at his feet. "I must've been seeing things, is all."

"You're a ghost hunter, but you don't believe your sister's spirit appeared to you with a message?"

His hands slide into his pockets again, and he blinks back tears. "I'm only in Lia's club because..."

"Because what?" she pipes up.

"It's you." He looks at her from under his bangs. "I like you."

This pronouncement flusters her. She tries to cover it with anger. "You don't believe in ghosts?"

A shoulder shrugs. "Not really. I want to because you do, but they sort of freak me out."

Sage nudges her with her elbow. Lia sets down her cup and muffin on the small veranda table. "I don't believe this."

Is she talking about the fact he admitted he likes her or the confession about ghosts? "You swear you put the crystal ball back after you got the message from your sister?" I ask.

He makes a pleading gesture with his hands. "I swear! I wanted to ask it if Lia would go to the spring formal with me."

"Even though you don't believe in this stuff," Kit says sarcastically.

"It's the first time I've asked anyone to a dance." He drops his hands, but his eyes are still pleading. Not with me this time, but with Lia. "I was really nervous. I was afraid you'd say no."

She stalks away, shaking her head. Travis looks defeated. I check my watch. "Lia, we need to get going, and you two need to talk. Why don't you catch up with us later?"

"No." She storms back and pokes him in the chest again. "You should have told me."

He flinches. "I know. I'm sorry. I didn't want to ruin our friendship."

"Well, you almost did." She puts her hands on her hips. "The dance is next weekend."

His face brightens. "Yeah?"

"I don't have time to get a dress."

He deflates. "Oh."

"Next time, you need to ask at least six to eight weeks in advance, got it?"

"Next time?"

She raises her chin. "I'll see what I can find in my closet for this one. After that, if you don't give me proper warning, I'll go with someone else."

"You're..." He motions at her, then at himself. "You'll go with me?"

"I'm super disappointed you're a nonbeliever, especially after seeing your sister, but we're still friends."

"Oh." He looks at me, somewhat confused. "Right. Friends."

"We'll see how next Saturday night at the dance goes," she tells him, snagging her coffee and muffin. "Maybe we'll be more."

His grin is electric. "Really? You forgive me?"

"Not yet, but you'll make it up to me."

"When you were at the booth," Logan interjects, uncrossing his ankles and boosting off the railing. "Did you notice anyone else hanging around or showing interest in the ball?"

Travis and Lia are heading down the steps, and he glances back. "Just that one gal."

Kit comes to stand beside me. "Which one?"

"She was wearing a pink cardigan. She kept pacing back and forth in front of the booth when I was trying to get close to the ball. You were talking to Mrs. Rosenfelt behind the table and had your back turned. I thought I wouldn't be able to get to the ball and back to class on time because she kept getting in my way."

We all exchange a look. "Pink cardigan?" I ask. "You don't know who she is?"

He shook his head. "But I think she has a table on the flea market side."

"Would you recognize her if you saw her again?" Logan asks.

He gives another one-shoulder shrug. "Maybe."

"Let's go," I say, rounding everyone up again. "I need to talk to her."

SEVEN

Several volunteers I've recruited from the library are waiting for us at the gate. Greeting them, I unlock it to let us all in. They gather around while I hand out assignments and then scatter to their assigned locations.

Daddy and Brax are in the announcer's booth in the bleachers. They meet me halfway down the stairs, and I hand each of them one of the coffees we brought. Brax tells me he has to get home to help Rhys with their overnight B&B guests and kisses the top of my head before jogging off. Looking tired, Daddy sips and tucks a pack of playing cards into his back pocket.

"Quiet night? I ask, hopeful.

He takes another sip. "Boring as could be. Around eleven, we had a group of teenagers climbing the fence, but I used my bullhorn and chased them off."

"You still have that old thing from your days on the force?"

He looks at me as if I'm dense. "You never know when you're going to need one."

But, of course. Everyone should have one on hand, right? "Where's your other helper?"

"Hank wasn't much good after about two, so I sent him home. Brax and I traded off taking cat naps."

Queenie is opening the awning on the food truck, and Brax stops to say hi before heading for the gate.

"Get some breakfast," I tell Daddy, "Queenie can put it on my tab. I really appreciate this."

He hugs me. "Your mother was still texting me at midnight. She's upset about what happened. Any more ideas on who the culprit might be?"

Travis is helping Lia set out a fresh stack of maps, tote bags, and T-shirts. "Maybe for the crystal ball, but I'm not sure about the other items. Do you think Jones is taking it seriously? This could put a black mark on my endeavor."

"Don't you worry." He pats my arm. "After I get a few winks, I'll return and start nosing around. Someone had to see something. By the way, the school has security cameras pointed at the entrances and parking lots. It's a long shot, but maybe they caught your thief on camera."

"That's brilliant."

"The only problem is, the school board won't offer up the recordings voluntarily. You might need a court order to get your hands on them."

My enthusiasm drops. "They might to prove it wasn't a student, right?"

"Doubtful. Still, I'll mention it to Landon. Your mom, too. They each have a lot of pull with certain community members." He winks.

We amble down the last few steps, and I scope the entire field as vendors begin to pour in. It looks like most of them are here, which is a relief. I stop on the last riser, hands on hips, searching for any in a pink cardigan. It's chilly but warming up fast, and I don't spot any sweaters, jackets, or long sleeves, period. "Thanks again, Daddy. Get yourself some breakfast and sleep. Keep me updated if you learn anything from Jones."

He hugs me and heads for Queenie's. I hustle to the welcome table and grab my clipboard. "Have you seen the woman from yesterday?" I ask Travis.

"I don't think so." He scratches the back of his head, his gaze darting around. "But there's so many of them already."

Logan points to the flea market layout on the top map. "Which table was she manning? Do you remember that?"

Travis studies it and shakes his head. "There were a lot of folks here yesterday. I'm not even sure if she was at a table. I mean, I think she was behind one when I saw her, but I was so freaked out about seeing my sister I wasn't paying that much attention when I went past her. I just wanted to get back to school."

Lia scoffs. "You must have been totally panicked if you, of all people, wanted to go back to our soul-sucking education system."

I feel bad for the boy and squeeze his shoulder. "I need to make rounds and check in with each seller. How about you go with me? Maybe seeing her behind her table today will spark your memory."

Logan produces a second clipboard, complete with a pen. "Travis and I will take the flea market. You check with the other side."

My seasoned soldier breaking down the work into manageable chunks. No wonder I love this guy. "Sounds like a plan. I want to question the booth owners on either side of Kit's. See if they noticed anyone paying unusual attention to her table."

Logan pulls out his phone and waggles it at me. "I'm a text away. If you get a lead, let me know pronto."

"Yes, sir. Ditto." Kit and Sage are in their spaces, and not surprisingly, I notice an orange cat slinking between them. "How did she get here?" I ask, more to myself than the others.

Logan and Travis walk off, and I notice the bald man from the previous day sauntering about with a camera around his neck. "What's he doing in here? He's not a vendor or flea market seller."

Lia follows my gaze. "That's a reporter from the *Thornhollow Tribune*," Lia says. She fumbles through her assortment of stuff on the table and hands me a business card. "He wants to interview some of the vendors for a human interest piece. He told me he'd like to talk to you, too."

A human interest piece, huh? Dollars to donuts, he wants to write about our missing items. That could be the final nail in my coffin. "Next time a reporter shows up, speak to me before you let them in."

"Did I do something wrong? I thought it would be a good thing to get some press."

"You're fine," I assure her. "But let me handle further media requests."

She snaps off a salute, her short pigtails bobbing. "Got it, boss."

There are already a few early-morning shoppers lining

up at the gate. Several call out greetings, and I return them before I march over to confront the reporter. He must be new—I don't recognize him.

When he sees me, he steps back and fiddles with something in his hand. It looks like a black plastic box. I hold out my hand to shake. "Hi, I'm Ava. Can I help you with something?"

His grip is firm, but he's nervous. He tucks the item behind his back and strokes the camera. "I'm Craig Lewis from the *Trib*. Just doing an article on the market."

"Then I'm the gal to talk to." I force a smile and hand him a flyer from my clipboard. "We want to support our local farmers, crafters, and small businesses under a year old—this explains it and gives you a list of those here. Thornhollow has a lot to offer our community members, as well as those in surrounding towns. Our vision is to go bigger over the next five years, and if things go as planned, we may even have a permanent building with monthly, if not weekly, events like this one." I wait for him to pull out a recorder or notebook. He does neither. "We want to add a monthly concert, a pet-centered day, a car show—you name it. The sky's the limit."

Scrutinizing the brochure, his lips press into a thin line. "That all sounds real nice," he finally says, sugary sweet with a bitter undertone, "but it seems you have a security problem, Mrs. Fantome-Cross. What are you doing about it?"

Bingo. I was right. It's not a human interest piece—he's stirring the drama pot. That's what sells newspapers. "This is our inaugural market, and there will be a few kinks. The situation has already been addressed, and next year, we'll have a full security team in place."

"Any leads on who stole from those poor vendors?"

I count to ten—okay, five—before responding like Mama taught me to do in order to control my temper. "We have several, in fact."

He scratches his chin. "Funny because, according to Detective Jones, there are none. Plenty of accusations, though. You've been pointing fingers at high school students, I hear?"

Kit walks up behind him and grabs what he's hiding out of his hand. She holds up his cell phone. A voice memo is recording everything we say. "What do we have here? Recording her without her knowledge? That's a bit under-handed, don't you think?"

Flustered, his lips thin again before he starts making excuses. "I don't have to divulge what I'm doing. I'm a reporter. Getting the scoop is what I do."

"I'm calling Mr. Lee at the paper," I tell Craig. "I very much doubt he'll approve of you trying to disgrace our market before it's even got its feet under it." I tap the flyer. "This is a good thing for our community, and while it's encountered a bump in the road, we're addressing it, and Magnolia Market will be twice as safe and twice as big next year."

"Walker Lee is my uncle," he informs me with a lift of his chin. "He wants a story, and I'm getting him one."

Kit taps buttons on the phone, and Craig tries to snatch it from her. "Sorry," she says with no remorse. "I accidentally erased whatever you had there. I'm so bad with technology."

He yanks it from her and stomps off.

"There goes my good publicity," I say.

She puts an arm around my shoulders. "He's a hack, and

no one reads the Tribune, anyway. Come on. You wanted to talk to the vendors next to me. Let's go do it."

"How did you know?"

She gives me the same look Daddy did about his bull-horn as she marches me toward her booth. "Psychic, remember?"

"You're not reading my mind *all* the time, are you?"

She grins and winks. "Don't be silly. You're an incredible person, but your mind is a chaotic mess."

"At least, I haven't seen Edith. On the other hand, neither have I seen my so-called guardian angel." Persephone has ignored all of my summons. "I even pleaded with her before I fell asleep last night. She's as stubborn as I am."

She chuckles. "I think she's got you beat on that front. And Edith is the spirit who doesn't want her granddaughter to sell her things?"

"The very one."

Kit resumes her place behind her table, arranging tiny crystals and tarot decks she has for sale. "I'm sorry I can't get a hit on the ball or who stole it."

"I know. We'll figure it out. Since Persephone won't help me, I'm calling in the big guns."

Kit raises a curious brow.

"Aunt Willa," I tell her. "She hasn't responded to my request for her to join us today and help me solve this mystery, but I have the feeling she will."

"Good." Kit smiles and gives a reassuring nod. "The more you ask for help, the more likely she is to grant it."

The owner to her left is Joe, the soap guy. "Nah," he says, shaking his head when I ask about the previous day. "I didn't see anyone toying with it, but I'm real sorry it's missing. Wilhelmina was always a sweet lady."

I thank him and move to the booth owner to Kit's right. "Hi, Susan. I know I checked in with you yesterday about the theft, but did you happen to remember anything overnight? Did you notice anyone paying particular atten- tion to Kit's table, especially while she was busy with a client?"

"No, not that I recall." She has a selection of journals that she's created from old books, vintage photographs, and miscellaneous items, such as buttons, ribbons, and more. "It was a busy day. I nearly sold out. I spent most of last night making a few more of my journals. Next year, I'll be sure to have at least twenty to thirty extras."

"I'm glad you're doing so well, and I hope you sell out today."

"Me, too. My sister did well yesterday, too. She's over in the flea market, selling some of the items she's bought at estate sales. That girl comes home with more than she can resell, and she'll probably take twice as much home from the market this weekend than she gets rid of." She gives a small laugh. "But it keeps her out of trouble, you know? She's really into all that"—she gestures at Kit's table—"occult stuff. Collects everything she can get her hands on."

"Is that so? Did she have a reading with Kit yesterday?"

Susan waves it off. "She was considering it. She kept coming over and stalking about but didn't pull the trigger, as they say. She's probably afraid to find out what her future looks like. Mama always said she'd never amount to much, believing in all that crazy woo-woo stuff."

"Was she wearing a pink cardigan yesterday?"

"That old thing? Our mother made it ages ago. Ugliest thing I ever saw."

Travis rushes up. "I found her. The woman. She's over there with a table of junk. Logan said to come get you."

Kit joins me at that moment. "Did you find it?"

It's like she has ESP or something. "Not yet, but we have a lead. Thanks, Susan," I say.

She's already rearranging her journals. "Sorry I couldn't be of any help."

Oh, but you have been.

Travis, Kit, and I rush to the flea market, and my hope is once more rising. She may have just helped us solve this mystery.

EIGHT

"Finally," Edith says, popping in right in front of me. "It's about time you talk to Sadie."

I pull up short, and my two companions also come to a halt and look at me funny.

Travis glances between me and the flea market gathering. "She's over there." He points.

Kit has heard Edith, and she waves him off. "Give us a second. We have to deal with a ghost."

The kid's face falls. "There's a ghost?"

He says it loud enough to attract attention from the closest tables. Several of the sellers look our way.

I motion for him to keep it down. "Pretend you're listening to me," I instruct.

Kit faces me while Travis backs away, bumping into a woman carrying a blue tub. "I think I'm gonna go find Lia," he announces over her chastising him.

Edith floats in my face. "Well? What are you waiting for?

She's selling off my collection of enchanted jars to one of the vintage vendors. You have to stop her!"

"Enchanted jars?" I echo. Kit and I exchange a glance. "You dabbled in magic?"

The ghost throws her hands skyward. "What does that matter? Those jars are beautiful, and they are specifically designed to hold elixir. I bought them from a shop in New Orleans twenty years ago. You can't find artistry like that anymore."

"What type of elixirs?" Kit asks.

Edith flaps around in a circle, kicking up a breeze that lifts strands of my hair. "Are you idiots? You don't know what an elixir is for?"

This is getting us nowhere. "Let's go see Sadie," I say to Kit. "Then we'll visit Connie."

By the time we get to Sadie's table, she's already made the deal with Jeremy Brune. He's gathering three colorful glass jars decorated with crystals into his arms. "Nice doing business with you," he says to her.

She preens, folding a stack of bills and sticking them in a pocket. "I've got more of that old junk back at my place if you wanna come over and have a look. I'll sell it to you dirt cheap."

I have the feeling that's not the only thing she wants to give him. He winks, seeming to think the same thing. "Maybe after closing tonight. We can go for a beer. Then swing by your place later?"

"You tell her that he's not good enough for her," Edith demands of me.

"I hate to interrupt this...conversation," I say, running a

finger over a jar. My skin tingles where it touches the glass. I pull back. "Can I speak to you a moment alone, Sadie?"

She gives me a sour scan from head to toe. "I'm kind of busy here, Ava." She clears her throat, and when she returns her attention to Jeremy, her lips morph into a lazy smile. Her eyes widen seductively. "I would love that."

"Stupid girl," Edith snarls. "Why, if I was still alive..."

"But you're not," Kit says. She nudges Jeremy to be on his way. "Sadie will catch up with you later, Romeo."

Jeremy and Sadie act flustered, and he croons over his shoulder at her, "I'll see you later."

Sadie waves at him and sighs. "Isn't he good enough to eat?" She makes a growling noise in her throat. "Yum."

Oh, good grief. "Did your grandmother have tarot cards, crystal balls, herbs, and elixirs?"

Sadie drags her attention to me and Kit. "She wasn't a witch, if that's what you're asking. She was just eccentric. A hoarder, too. Like, oh my god, you should see all the knick-knacks and collections she had. It's ridiculous."

"Eccentric!" Edith circles us again, the cover of one of her herbal books flips open, and the pages flutter in the breeze. "She doesn't even know what that word means. Why, I have more magic in my little finger"—she holds up her pinky, ghostly pale and transparent—"than that girl has in her entire body."

"I'm sure you do," I say to Edith.

"Huh?" Sadie asks.

I take a deep breath, close my eyes to rearrange my facial features, and pop them back open to smile at her. In my peripheral vision, I see Logan approaching. "Sadie, you probably don't know this, but I'm a medium. I can speak to ghosts."

I've lowered my voice, and she leans forward in order to hear me. Her eyes widen again, this time in surprise. "You mean like that Long Island gal on TV?"

Persephone is probably laughing right now. "I don't normally approach people in public, but your grandmother is insistent that I pass on a message to you."

She rears back, her gaze dinging around. "My grandmother? She's here?"

"She's here, all right," Kit tells her. "And she's angry. She's causing quite a ruckus and driving Ava up the wall."

Sadie scrutinizes my friend. "You're the psychic. You..." She points from Kit to me. "You talk to ghosts, too?"

Kit doesn't go into the specifics. "Your grandmother doesn't like you selling her things. She wants you to stop. If you understand the sentimentality she associates with them, she'll cross over, content that she's left her possessions in good hands."

"Thanks," I murmur to Kit as Sadie frowns.

"Seriously?" the gal asks.

Edith rolls her eyes and gets in Sadie's face. "You don't have the sense God gave a green apple."

"Your grandmother loves you," I tell the woman. "She wants you to be happy, but she also feels that all the stuff she left you has meaning and wants you to respect it."

Logan touches my elbow. When I glance at him, he gives a small smile of encouragement. He knows I don't want to do this, and he knows the reasons why. He's been supportive, unlike almost everyone else, but I know he believes I'm destined to do this, whether I want to or not.

"Your grandmother believes her items should stay in the family, Sadie," I continue, scanning those she still has for sale. "Are all of these things hers?"

She waves a hand over them. "What am I going to do with all this stuff? I don't have room for it, and it's helping me pay my bills. What I should do is give it all to Jeremy and let him sell it for me."

Edith screeches and sails through the air at her. She goes right through Sadie, but her granddaughter loses her balance and grabs at the table to keep from falling. Logan and I instinctively reach for her, but she and the table topple to the ground.

Everything ends up scattered on and around her. "Good grief," she grunts. Staggering to her feet, she visibly shudders. "I don't feel so good. All this talk about my grandmother."

She blinks a few times, watching Logan straighten her table. Kit picks up a few items, and I can tell by how she freezes before returning them to their places that she's gotten a hit.

Her brows furrow. "You've sold some of Edith's things to the other vendors besides Jeremy, haven't you?"

"Sure." Sadie grips the edge of the table. Her face is pale, her gaze unfocused. "That's what flea marketers do. They go to estate sales, buy stuff dirt cheap, and then circulate through the various markets to resell it."

Kit touches my arm. "The other missing items. That's the connection. They belonged to Edith."

"They still belong to me," the ghost insists, pointing at her scrawny chest.

I nearly jump for joy at this revelation, except Aunt

Willa's crystal ball has no tie to Edith. Does it? I can see that Kit is wondering the same thing.

Logan, also on board, asks, "Was your grandmother friends with Wilhelmina Duchamp?"

Sadie does a Travis impression, shrugging a shoulder and sliding her hands into her pockets. I can see her fingering the bills from Jeremy. "She was friends with a lot of people. It's a small town. She always did claim she knew everyone around."

Just like Mama and Edith had said she knew her. She must have known Aunt Willa, too. But how did that connect to the crystal ball?

"Of course, I knew Willa," Edith growls. "She thought she was better than me, but she was small time when it came to using magic. Helping folks with love potions and house clearings." She makes a dismissive noise. "Elias and I were building an empire with ours."

"Who's Elias?" I ask.

Sadie thinks I'm talking to her. "That old geezer? He's weird. Like, horror-movie weird. She called him her *para-mour*." Revulsion screws up her face. "He's a Grade A creep."

"Is he here?" I ask. "Does he have a booth?"

Another shrug, and she pulls her hands out of her pockets. "He's a collector." She uses quotes around the word. "He's a hoarder like grandma. He probably keeps his own fingernail clippings. I thought I saw him yesterday, but if he was here, he wouldn't have come to see me. Thank God."

"Who else here at the market has some of your grandmother's items for sale?" Logan asks.

"Carl Anderson, Lorna Cummings..." Her eyes grow big as the truth hits home. "Oh, for heaven's sake. The stolen items. They were all hers."

Logan pulls me a step away and lowers his voice. "Her grandmother isn't stealing them back, is she?"

Anything is possible, and Edith is incredibly strong for a ghost, but I doubt it. "Hey, Edith," I softly ask the ghost. "You haven't taken back your things from the people Sadie sold them to, have you?"

She puts her hands on her hips, and once again, I feel like I need to avert my eyes from the display behind the fabric of her nightgown. "Are you stupid, girl? Do you think if I had *that* kind of power, I would let her sell them in the first place? They were supposed to help me become immortal or at least make the afterlife better than this." She glances skyward in a vague sense of disgust. "But here I am, dead as a doorknob. The afterlife is dull as dishwater."

If Mama heard her, she would correct both idioms: dead as a doornail, dull as ditchwater. "Technically, you haven't moved on to the afterlife," I tell her. Sadie follows my gaze to the point I'm staring at. "And you need to. You can't stay earthbound without consequences."

Sadie props her hands on the table and leans forward once again. "Is she haunting me? What kind of consequences?"

If only I could handle one of them at a time...

My phone buzzes with a text from Lia. *It's time to open, and there's a big crowd. What do you want me to do?*

Hurriedly, I reply. *I'll send Logan.* To him, I say, "It's eight already. I need you at the gate."

"I'm on it." He squeezes my arm. "You can handle this."

As he jogs away, Kit says, "I'm afraid I have to abandon you, too."

"I know. It's okay."

She gives a wink and heads off. I turn to the ghost. I need to wrap this up quickly. "Edith, you're no longer part of this plane of existence. It's time for you to move on and let Sadie live her life."

Sadie straightens. "What if I keep the rest of the stuff? Will that make you happy, Nana?"

Edith hesitates, then shakes her head. "She has to collect the things she sold and return them to my home. I willed the house to her, so I know she has plenty of space."

People flood across the field toward us. "It appears the only way your grandmother is going to be happy is if you collect all of her possessions and return them to her place," I inform Sadie.

"I can't do that." She bites her bottom lip. "*Should* I do that?"

"It's your decision. I'll do my best to cross your grand-mother to the afterlife, but right now, I have a market to run. If I were you, I would pack up her stuff and call it a day. Once we get things worked out with her spirit, then you can move forward with selling things."

"You really stink at this," Edith says, and then she vanishes.

"Tell me about it," I mutter.

"What?" Sadie asks.

I shake my head. "Nothing. I'll talk to you again later."

I wheel around and speak to several folks on my way to Connie's table. Her mother sits in a folding chair off to the side, knitting needles in action as another sweater takes shape, this one bright orange. Connie is bent over a plastic container, pulling out some gothic-looking candle holders. "Good morning," I say.

Her mom glances up and gives me a nod while Connie turns with the items in hand, a bright smile on her face. When she sees it's me, the smile fades. "Can I help you with something?"

"You're not wearing that pretty pink cardigan," I say with false interest. "It caught my eye yesterday."

She fidgets with the candle holders, avoiding eye contact, and then smoothes the royal blue cotton tablecloth under them. "It's a prize, that's for sure. Mom's creations are one of a kind."

Her mother beams with pride. "Next year, I'm going to sell them here. You put me down for a booth in the craft section, will ya?" She adjusts her yarn. "Want me to make you one? This is for Susan, but I can start on yours as soon as I finish it. What color should I make?" She fixes me with a look. "Red, I think. A cheery Christmas shade."

"Oh, gosh, that's kind of you." I'm pretty sure I'm not a red cardigan person. I decide to get to the point before we're overrun with shoppers. "My friend, Kit, noticed you at her booth yesterday, Connie, and as you may have heard, my aunt's crystal ball is missing. I was wondering if you saw anyone with it."

Tabby saunters up at that moment, leaping onto the table and startling Connie. "You get off my table!" She flaps a hand at her. "Shoo! Go away!"

Tabby flexes her paws and sinks her claws into the cloth, then leaps down, taking the material with her.

The women scream, and items fly everywhere. Connie

stumbles into her mom, and when the table falls over, a pair of the plastic storage containers that she'd stored under it are revealed.

On top of one rests an item that sparkles in the sunlight. At the sight of the crystal, my breath catches in my chest.

NINE

Unless Aunt Willa's crystal ball drank Alice in Wonderland's shrinking potion, the one I'm staring at is not hers.

It catches the sunlight perfectly, however, sending a pointed ray toward my chest. The spot immediately warms right through my shirt.

"You horrible feline," Connie shouts, gaining her feet and shaking her finger at Tabby, who trots off with her tail high. "You better hope I don't catch you!"

If only she knew who the cat actually is. Catching her would be a horrible idea.

I help Connie fix the table. "Are you okay?" I ask.

She shakes out the cloth and spreads it across the top once more. "You better call animal control."

Her mother gains her feet and stares at the jumble of knotted thread tangled with her knitting needles. "My, my, I've got my work cut out for me now. I think I dropped at least four stitches."

Connie doesn't ask after her, only snaps a finger and points at the scattered items on the ground. "Help me get these back on the table!"

Her mother sets the chair back up and places the yarn on the seat. "All right, all right. Keep your pants on."

"I noticed you have a crystal ball in one of your containers," I say. "Pretty little thing. Do you have any bigger?"

"I collect them," she tells me, rearranging items as her mother hands them to her, and folks walk by. "I have over fifty at home."

"Is that so? Where do you keep them all?" I don't care, I just want to keep her talking about them.

An interested customer steps up beside me, eyeing a selection of metal charms stamped with sigils and symbols. Connie pastes on a smile and asks if there is something in particular the gal is looking for.

She appears to be in her thirties, with streaks of red in her hair and a nose piercing. "I'm a poet, and I'm searching for a talisman to boost my creativity and help me find success with a contest I've entered."

"Oh." Connie bites her bottom lip and runs a finger over several of the pewter pendants with their black cords. "This one." She picks an interesting design. "It's a magical seal. All you have to do is set your intention and then wear it whenever you're writing."

The potential customer studies it, rubbing the bead that connects the pendant to the cord between her thumb and finger. "How much?"

"I'll give you a deal since I love poetry. That one alone is thirty, but if you buy two, they're twenty apiece."

The woman regards the rest of the collection, holding

onto the item she believes will help her. She uses a finger to touch each of the others, returning to one with several beads and a sigil with multiple points. "What does this mean?"

"That's to call in a guardian angel. If you need protection or want help, that's the one for you."

Huh. I wonder if it would work for me. *Persephone*, I mentally call to her, *I'm going to replace you.*

I wish, comes her reply.

"I'll take it." The woman fishes in her pocket for money. "It's for my sister."

While they finish their transaction, I try not to look at my watch. I have so many things to do, and I need to check in with the farmers and crafters, but I don't want to let the crystal ball discussion wait.

"If I get my book of poetry printed," the customer tells Connie, "I'll bring you a signed copy."

Connie seems genuinely happy at the prospect. Maybe she is. Either way, she's a skilled salesperson and wishes the customer good luck before the woman moves on. The smile falls off her face when she turns her attention back to me. "Is there something else?"

The way to win her over is to buy something. I point to the container under the table. "I don't suppose that crystal ball is for sale?"

It takes her a second to remember what we were discussing before the interruption. "I bought that yesterday for my collection. It's not available ."

"Who did you get it from?"

"Sadie Haversham, but she doesn't have anymore. The psychic on the other side of the market has a giant one. I wanted to ask if she would consider selling it since I've never seen one that big. Every time I went to ask, though, she was busy with a client."

My heart sinks. "You wanted to buy it?"

"I doubt she'd part with it, and it's probably way more than I can afford, but...I can't stop thinking about it. It would be the crowning glory of my set."

If she's acting, she's very convincing. "When you were over by Kit, the psychic, did you notice anyone else hanging around that seemed interested in it?"

She tilts her head and gives me a curious look. "It was getting a lot of attention. Probably still is. Why?"

"You haven't heard? It was stolen."

Her mouth falls open. "You are kidding! Oh no. I can't believe it. How could someone take off with something so big?"

"You're sure you didn't notice anyone toying with it?"

"She had a line of people waiting for a reading every time I was there. It was a busy section between her, the soap guy, and the woman offering shoulder massages." She pulls her shoulders up to her neck and releases them. "I wanted to see her, too, but there was no break in the action."

One of Thornhollow's newest service providers is Delinda Hawkins. A masseuse also certified in the ancient art of Reiki, she's already building a solid clientele. When she lived and worked closer to Atlanta, she had a massage chair and did upper body massages at a mall. When she applied to do them at the market, I knew she would be a unique and popular addition. "Thanks anyway. If you think of anything else, please let me know."

"I heard about some other stuff that got stolen. I guess I'm pretty lucky. The thief didn't hit my booth."

Her mother has returned to the chair and is working on the knots. "They know better than to come here. I'll poke them with my needles."

With her back to her mother, Connie gives me an eye roll. "We'll be on the lookout. I'll holler if we spy anyone with it."

I leave her and meander past several other stalls, questioning the sellers. They all want to talk, but luckily, there are enough customers that none keep me too long. Unfortunately, none offer any insight into our stolen goods, either.

I'm heading toward the food trucks, determined to grab a snack and a coffee before tackling my list, when Edith appears. "I talked to your spirit guide again. She says you won't help me."

"If you want help, it's quid pro quo."

This gets her attention, and she hovers closer. I ignore the strange looks I get from a couple who pass us, wondering why I'm talking to myself. "What's that supposed to mean?" Edith asks.

I motion her to a spot between two food trucks, where we're less conspicuous. "You've been nothing but rude, and you're not trying to see this from your granddaughter's perspective. Why would she want to live in your house with all your possessions? She's young, and she needs help paying her bills. Selling your stuff will do that. She doesn't need a shrine to you, and if you want to stay connected to her, don't use your possessions in order to do it. You seem to be more worried about them than you are about her."

Edith blinks, for once at a loss for words.

"If you haven't noticed, I'm still alive, like Sadie," I continue. "I'm a bit busy running this market. While I live in

Willa's house and took over her event planning business, my connection to her is far more important than any of her possessions. You need to shift your priorities."

Offended, she peers down her nose at me. This is easier for her to do since she's floating several feet off the ground. "What do you want"?"

Now we're getting somewhere. "First off, be kinder to me and Sadie. Secondly, cross over to the afterlife. Trust me, once you're there, you won't care about your house or possessions any longer."

"I agree to the first part, but not to the second. How do I know what's waiting for me on the other side? I love my house and things. I don't know what I'll find over there."

How can I convince her? "I'm sure you have family and friends waiting for you. Don't you want to be reunited with them?"

She snorts. "My parents didn't care about anyone but themselves. And I could count my friends on one hand. Some of them are still here, at least the fun ones."

"We'll revisit that later, but there's not much I can do to convince Sadie to keep your stuff. She's already sold a lot and seems determined to get rid of the rest. Is there something in particular that you'd like her to keep as a tribute to you?"

She pauses. "Well, she should hang onto that set of cookbooks she's bound up with twine and has underpriced. When she was a girl, she stayed with me often, and we made meals together from those recipes. Like a journal, I wrote dates and little tidbits next to the ones we made. She probably doesn't remember, but if she would open them and look inside, she'd see my notes. They might mean something to her."

"What a lovely thing for her to keep. I'll do my best to convince her to keep them, but I need you to do something for me."

"I said I'd be nicer."

"But you didn't agree to the second part of the deal, so here's an alternative. My aunt's crystal ball has gone missing, and I need to know who stole it so I can get it back. "

"How do you think I can help with that?"

"You're a ghost. The other stolen items are all connected to you, and it's a strong possibility that the thief who took them also took that ball. Use some of your mojo and figure out where they went. Your energy is stored in them, so you should be able to find them. When you do, tell me who's got them, and I'll make sure to get them back."

Making deals with spirits is a fifty-fifty game, but since I don't have Persephone to drop any of her cryptic clues on me, and I haven't seen her ghostly boyfriend, Sherlock, who's an ace at solving mysteries, I have to make do with what I have. That means Edith.

"You think I can find the missing items?" she asks.

"It might take you a couple of tries, and you can certainly ask Persephone for help, but yes." If my guardian angel isn't helping me, maybe she'll help Edith. Persephone certainly has tried to use her to get me back in the game. Turnabout seems like fair play. "Don't be surprised if she refuses, but you seem to have a way of bossing people around. Don't let her blow you off."

Edith smirks. "She'll help me."

She disappears, and I look longingly at Queenie's food truck, smelling the aroma of baked goods and coffee streaming from it. Putting my needs on hold, I return to

Sadie and wait until she's done with a customer before I can talk to her. "You're back," she says.

Here goes nothing. "Your grandmother wants you to look in that stack of cookbooks." I point to the set with the telltale twine around them and a tag reading seven dollars. "When you were young, you stayed with her and made recipes from those. She claims she put notes in the margins—little tidbits about the things you did together. She wants you to keep those as a tribute to her. Will you do that for me? I'll give you ten dollars if you just keep them."

"I remember." A soft smile plays over her lips, softening her features. "Gosh, that was a long time ago. Some of the meals were terrible." She chuckles. "But some of them were pretty good. Nana always fiddled with the recipes when she didn't have all the right ingredients."

"I'm sure her notes will bring back more memories."

She holds out her hand. "I'll take that ten bucks."

So much for reminiscing. I dig a bill from my pocket and hand it to her, satisfied that I've held up my end of the bargain.

I'm on my way to Queenie's when my phone rings. It's Daddy.

"I thought you might want to know," he tells me. Landon's checked all the local pawn shops and eBay. No one has tried to sell the stolen items yet."

"I have new information for him. All of the items, with the exception of the crystal ball, were part of Edith Haversham's estate. I suspect our thief knew her when she was alive, although I don't know what they want with those specific items or why they didn't offer to buy them if they have sentimental value."

"I'll pass that on. Do you need me tonight to keep an eye on things?"

"No sales on Sunday. Everyone will be packing up this evening. The food trucks are using the bus lanes to offer brunch from ten to one tomorrow, and the free concert is at three." Which he knows since he's one of the performers. It hits me then—once they pack up and leave, I've lost every potential trail to our thief. "Any chance I can borrow you this afternoon? I still haven't had breakfast, and I want to question those we can again."

"I'll be there in an hour. Go get something to eat."

"Thanks, Daddy."

I am thwarted once again, however, when Lia staggers up to me, her eyes red and her face splotchy. She's crying. "Oh, Ava, everything is a mess."

"What happened?"

She throws her arms around my waist and sobs. "I screwed it all up."

"What?"

She hiccups. "Wrenlee. She hates me now."

I pat her back. "What? Why?"

"It's all over that stupid dance." She lifts her tear-stained face. "You have to help me, Ava. She's my best friend. Ever. And she says"—she hiccups and starts crying harder.

"She says what?"

Her shoulders shake, tears falling on her shirt. "She says she's never going to talk to me again! What am I going to do?"

TEN

My dream of getting something to eat fades quickly. I wrap an arm around her shoulders. "Tell me what happened."

She releases her grip, dashing away tears from her cheeks. "I didn't know. She never told me."

"Told you what?"

Her chest heaves, and her eyes flick toward the gate where Travis and Logan are manning the table. "She's in love with him."

I follow her gaze. "Travis?"

Her head bobs in confirmation. "He's crushing on me, and she's crushing on him." She hiccups again but contains her sob. "She freaked out when he told her that I said yes about going to the dance with him. She thought he was going to ask her!"

Young love. Heck, even adults end up in tangled knots over it. My mind flashes back to Connie's mother and her knitting. No matter how you try to untangle a love triangle, there's no winning that battle. "Emotions are running high. Give her time. Her heart is broken right now, but it will mend."

She gives an exasperated flip of her hands. Her shoulders droop with the heavy load of her emotions. "The thing is, I like him a lot, but I'm not in love with him. I'm still kind of crushing on Carlyn. I mean, I know she's never going to fall in love with me, but..." She thumps a fist against her heart. "I can't seem to get over her, you know?"

I'm hardly an expert on relationships, but I know there's no fixing the situation at the moment. "Travis didn't realize that Wrenlee has feelings for him?"

She shakes her head. "She's not talking to him either. She won't return our texts or answer our calls. What should I do?"

I can't send her back to the table in this state, and she needs someone else to talk to who can offer suggestions. Someone who can calm her down. I ease her around and start toward Sage's booth. "At the moment, nothing. You can't change how Travis feels about you or how Wrenlee feels about him. You're caught in the middle of a situation that's not of your making, and the more you try to fix it, the worse it will get."

She leans against me as we walk, returning one arm to my waist. "I have to do *something*. I can't lose my best friend."

I'm torn between telling her it's already happened and holding out hope that Wrenlee will realize their friendship is more important than a boy. I squeeze her shoulder. "Take a deep breath and have Sage make you some of her Velvet Dreams tea. You're not thinking clearly right now, and neither is Wrenlee. You need time and perspective on the situation."

She wipes her eyes again. "Maybe Kit can predict the future and tell me what will happen. Can I ask her?"

As we pass the Younkers' stall, Pete hails me. "Could I speak to you, Ava? Privately?"

His wife's ghost hovers next to him. "Tell him! I know it's been two years, but tell him I'm still here," she insists.

I stiffen at her appearance. "One thing at a time," I say to Lia. "Talk to Sage. I'll be over in a few minutes."

Lia glances between Pete and me. She's highly perceptive, picking up on how I've tensed. "Is it ghost stuff?" she whispers.

I wish it wasn't, but it seems there's no avoiding it. "Sure is." I give her a nudge to move her along and smile at Pete. "Absolutely. Let's talk over at the goalpost."

Lia brightens. "Can I stay? Please? We haven't had a good story in a while for our vlog."

Luckily, Pete has already started for the end zone. It feels like the dead zone as Olivia waves at me to hurry up and join him. "It's a sensitive situation, so I best handle it alone and in private. You've got enough on your plate, anyway," I add. "If there's anything to report, I'll catch you up to speed later."

"But—"

"Go. Now."

Her shoulders sag once more. It's typical for her to worm her way into these things. She's passionate about ghost hunting. In this case, it's more about forgetting her problems and focusing on someone else's. I'm sorry to disappoint her but must respect Pete and Olivia's privacy.

I watch as she saunters off, and then I join the two of

them. My phone buzzes in my back pocket, but I ignore it. "What can I do for you?" I ask Pete.

He shifts his weight from foot to foot, glancing nervously at his girls who are staffing the booth." I've heard you're... You know."

I keep silent, not wanting to fill in the blank with the wrong answer. I am sure he's going to ask me about his wife, and yet, I'm holding out hope it's something else.

He stammers, digging the toe of his well-worn boot into the ground, then stopping himself. He smooths down the turf and looks embarrassed. "I think I feel my wife hanging around the farmhouse." It comes out in a rush. He sneaks a peek at me from the corner of his eye, then stares at the lawn again. "I know it sounds crazy, but it's like she's still there. She told me to move on before she passed, and it's been over two years, but...I smell her perfume, sometimes, and"—he shakes his head and chuckles. "I'm sorry. I don't know how to go about this."

Olivia starts in with a list of things for me to tell him. I begin with my own. "You're not crazy. And yes, you've heard right. I can help with your problem"—I correct myself— "*circumstances*, I mean."

This time, his glance lasts longer, his brow dipping over his eyes. "Is it a problem? It kind of feels...good. Like she's still around, helping me with the girls and the farm. Her favorite rosebush is blooming like crazy right now, and I swear it's because she always had a green thumb, you know? I look out the window all the time, and I can still see her bending over that thing, talking to it, and nurturing it. A tear leaks out the corner of his eye, and he brushes it away. "Man, I sound like a sap. I'm just so lonely."

Broken hearts—I wish I could soothe them all. Hugging my clipboard to my chest, my own heart breaking for him, I glance at his wife, who is now silent. "This is a delicate situation." It seems as if I am caught in one of those at every turn. "The thing is, Pete, she's earthbound. You do smell her perfume and hear her voice. You may even see her spirit at the rosebush."

"Really?" His face lights up, and his eyes are filled with unexpected joy. "I never believed in this stuff before, but I want to. I miss her so much." His voice catches, and tears prick my eyes.

I glance at the ghost and speak to her *and* him. "The problem is, she can't remain earthbound, or she'll become angry and hateful. The dead aren't supposed to linger here—this isn't their plain of existence."

He stops fidgeting. "I don't understand."

I don't always understand it myself. I try to explain as best as I can. "She needs to move onto the afterlife. That's where she belongs. She may be able to visit you and your girls once she's there to keep an eye on you, but you need to let her go. It's your love that keeps her anchored here, and while it's noble for her to stay because she knows you need her, it's not fair to any of you for her to be trapped in a world where she doesn't belong."

Olivia shakes her head. "I want to stay here."

Pete's lips turn up in a shaky smile. "She stayed because of us?"

This seems to please him, and I get it, but I have to convince him to let her go. She hovers near, whispering in his ear. No good can come from that. "Have you ever been in a place where you didn't belong?"

He shrugs. "Sure, my first job out of college. Corporate America is not for me."

I nod, noticing Persephone loitering around the trunk of the goalpost. Her brash smile says she's confident she has won this battle. Maybe she has. "At first, it may have seemed all right," I tell him. "Tolerable even. Eventually, however, you knew you didn't belong there and became frustrated, irritated, depressed, perhaps?"

"All of that and a whole lot more. I was determined to make it work, but it just didn't. I was never so happy as to get back to the farm."

"Then you can understand what happens to a spirit when it is trapped where it doesn't belong, right?"

Comprehension registers and the previous hope in his eyes fades. "You're sure? There's no way she can stay for a while?"

"It's my experience and understanding that ninety-nine percent of spirits who stay attached to this plane eventually go mad. Instead of her presence being welcoming in your home, you'll end up with a haunting. She'll be much harder to move on if that happens."

Olivia puffs up like an adder. "Stop telling that! I would never do such a thing. He and the girls need me! He's all alone."

I clutch my clipboard like a shield. She's not as strong as Edith, but I can feel her agitation blowing strands of hair back from my face.

As if they feel their mother's wrath as well, both girls turn to stare at us.

Pete strokes the back of his neck. "How can we help her?" he asks.

"She needs to go to the light."

"No!" Olivia tries to push me away, but her hands go through me. "Stop it! I'm not going anywhere."

I shudder at her cold energy. Normally, I can envision a doorway that leads to the afterlife, and most ghosts are drawn to it, but at the moment, with her shouting at me, I find my imagination skills lacking. "Knock it off," I say to her. To him, I suggest, "Perhaps I can visit you after the market is over? We can talk to the girls together, explain things, and then I can help Olivia cross."

He glances around. "Is she here?"

"Tell him," Olivia demands. "Tell him I love him."

"She is, and she says she loves you," I relate.

Relief dances on his face. "Tell her I love her, too."

"She can hear you." I watch as she whispers in his ear again and kisses his cheek.

He can feel it and raises his fingers to touch the spot.

She faces me again. "I won't go. He has no one. The girls need a mother."

To him, I say, "It would be a good idea for you to talk to Olivia and tell her that you and the girls will be okay without her. That she'll still be with you in your hearts and that you will always honor and love her."

He shoves his hands in his jeans pockets and scans the area, searching for her. His body language and aura are filled with sadness again. "Sure. I can do that."

"How about one evening next week?"

"Wednesday? The girls will be home from school around three-thirty."

"I'll be there."

"Well, I won't," Olivia says, then disappears.

"She's gone for now," I tell him. "We can talk to her more when I visit. Give you a chance to say your goodbyes."

He returns to his booth, wrapping his arms around his daughters.

Persephone materializes in front of me. "Good job, ghost whisperer."

I ignore her and head for Sage and Lia.

"Now, maybe things will get back to normal," she says, following. "We have quite a backlog to catch up on."

My phone rings. I pull it out, grateful for the distraction. It's Rosie. "Hey, how did the ceremony go? I bet Tessy looked beautiful."

"She did. The only problem is she only made it halfway down the aisle."

My heart sinks. "What happened? Did she pass out?"

It wouldn't be the first time. "Nope. She didn't pass out, she turned and ran."

I stop in my tracks. "What? You can't be serious."

It's as if I can feel her worrying the cross pendant that hangs at her neck with nervous fingers. "Dead serious. Ava, we have a runaway bride."

ELEVEN

I whirl, hustling for the gate. "Where did she go? Any ideas?"

"None," Rosie says. "Everyone is searching for her." I hear a car motor kick over as Rosie joins in the hunt. "Her family is devastated, and Reverend Stout is consoling them while her friends and I look for her. She's not answering calls, and we've already checked her normal hang-outs. Nada."

A splash of white on the bleachers catches my eye. Still in her gown, Tessy is seated halfway up the rows next to a man in a black hat and trench coat. "Wait. I've got her."

And maybe Elias, too.

"You *what*?" Rosie exclaims.

"She's here." I switch directions, hurrying toward the risers. "Let me talk to her and see if I can calm her down enough to return to the church and work this out with Brian. I'll call you back."

"You're sure?"

"Yep, just let her family know she's safe."

We disconnect, and I hear my name shouted from my left. "Ava!"

I slow and see Logan carrying a white container. "I got you a snack," he says with a triumphant smile. "You've got to eat."

This man. "Bless you. My stomach is so empty, I'm light-headed." I accept the foam carrier, my nose already scenting one of Queenie's bacon and egg biscuits. "You're a lifesaver."

I resume my path to the bleachers, and he falls into step with me. "Where are you going in such a rush?" he asks.

I pop the lid and grab the sandwich. Maybe I can get a couple of bites in before I reach Tessy. "I'm putting out fires that are popping up faster than I can blink." I use the sandwich to point at my bride and narrow my eyes when I realize the man is gone. Mentally, I curse. If he's Elias and our thief, he's eluded me. Maybe Tessy will know where he went. "I've got to talk her off the edge and get her back to the church to say 'I do.'"

He follows the direction of my makeshift pointer. "The Borage-Judson wedding? She left him at the altar?"

I quickly chew and swallow. "Maybe she decided that committing to a second round wasn't what she wanted."

"Do you want me to come with you?"

"I doubt there's much either of us can do. All I can do is see if there's hope she'll still go through with it. I'd kill for a cup of coffee, though." I gave him my best smile and bat my lashes.

"What happened to yours?"

"Not sure. It's been a crazy morning."

He gives the back of my neck a swift but gentle massage. "One coffee coming up. Good luck with your bride."

As he walks away, I down half the sandwich and contemplate what to say to Tessy. She's not going anywhere, so I slow my approach, climbing the bleachers while I finish my food. When she spots me, she rolls the chaplet beads in her hand between her fingers. Her grandmother gave it to her for her 'something borrowed.' It's been in their family for generations, and even though Tessy isn't Catholic, I know how much her grandmother means to her.

Her eyes are dry and clear, so she hasn't been crying. I ease down next to her, setting the foam container aside and wiping my mouth with the napkin provided. "I didn't expect to see you today."

"I admit, I'm embarrassed to be here."

"Wanna talk about it?"

She works the beads through her fingers as if praying for a miracle. Maybe she is. "I love Brian, I do. It's not that, but... We tried it once, and it didn't work. We have different wants, different goals. Things are easy with him, I'll give you that. He's handsome, independent, a good guy..."

I can't tell if she's trying to convince herself or me. "It's perfectly okay to change your mind."

Her gaze drifts across the field toward the farmers market. "I'm scared, Ava. I don't want to end up alone, but marrying Brian doesn't feel right. I want a family, and I'm not getting any younger."

There's a desperation in her tone. "He doesn't want kids?"

"That's why we divorced. Initially, he told me he was fine with it, but he got cold feet when I was ready to start trying. He said he enjoyed things the way they were. Today, when I was walking down the aisle, it felt like closing the door on that dream. There was such finality, I froze." She bends over and puts her face in her hands. "What am I doing? I've screwed up everything."

It's the second time I've heard that today. Across the way, I spot Lia running toward us, her hand waving at me as she carries a cup in the other. She looks excited. "Relationships are tough," I say to Tessy. "You have to talk to Brian and lay this all out on the table. Who knows? Maybe he'll be willing to reconsider."

Olivia appears two risers down from us. Her attention is locked on her husband and daughters. Pete is bagging up vegetables for a customer as their eldest accepts the payment. "She's still in love with Pete," Olivia says flatly. "Always has been."

This revelation shocks me. I glance at Tessy and see her peeking through her fingers at him in the distance.

"Do you know Pete Younkers?" I ask.

She startles, straightening and nearly dropping the chaplet. "What?" She chuckles nervously. "Sure. We went to school together. Dated for a while."

Oh, boy. Even though I'm not psychic, I see pieces of a grander picture lining up. "Why did you break up?"

She darts a glance at me from the corner of her eye, then looks away. "Olivia Williams. Her family moved to town when we were sophomores, and he fell head over heels for her. I never stood a chance."

I can see the side of Olivia's face. She's smiling at the

memory. "He never meant to hurt her," she tells me. "It was just love at first sight for both of us."

Lia dashes up the steps. "Hey, Ms. Borage! Aren't you getting married today?"

Tessy has been a middle school teacher for ten years. She inhales wistfully. "I had a change of plans. What do you have there?"

Lia sits at our feet and tips her cup so I can see the bottom. "Good news. Sage read my tea leaves, and everything's going to work out!"

"Tea leaves?" Tessy asks.

Lia nods vigorously, pointing to them. "I thought I'd screwed up with Travis and Wrenlee, but it looks like I can fix it. Sage says I have to remain true to myself and talk it out with the two of them. I like Travis a lot, but he's not right for me. We can be friends, sure, but my heart belongs to someone else. And whatever happens between him and Wrenlee is their business. I'm here to support them, of course, but I can't control how they feel about each other."

"From the mouths of babes," I mutter.

Olivia swivels to look at my young friend. The anger she expressed earlier is gone, replaced by a sadness I recognize. "No one can predict the future. How can that woman know that?"

"Sage is right," I say to all of them. "We can't control other people or the way they feel about us. We can't force them to love us or stop ourselves from loving them sometimes. All we can do is be faithful to ourselves and kind to everyone else."

Olivia disappears as Brian arrives, jogging up the aisle. When Tessy sees him, she tenses. "Oh, no."

I squeeze her arm. "You can do this. Be honest with him."

He stops a few feet from her and raises his hands. "What the heck, Tessy?"

She swallows hard and stands, facing him. "I'm sorry. I know I've disappointed you and our families. I wanted it to work, but I don't want to be eighty and look back and realize that I gave up my dream of having a family because I was scared of ending up alone." He drops his hands, and she moves toward him. "You're a special guy who deserves someone just as special. I want a family, and I deserve a husband who wants that, too. I hope you understand."

The emotions he's holding back are visible on his face. He looks out over the field, not seeming to see it, and a muscle in his jaw ticks. "But we're so good together. I don't want to lose you."

"We are," she agrees. "In every way, except for one. You're my best friend, and I hate to hurt you like this, but I've decided this is nonnegotiable. Family is important to me, and I want kids."

He sets one of his feet on the riser in front of him, the black leather shiny and new. "You're a teacher. You see kids every day at school. Isn't that enough?"

"It's not." She releases a heavy sigh and gestures at Lia. "I mean, I love my students, but it's not the same, Brian."

"You'll make a great mom," Lia tells her.

Brian shoots Lia a stern look, and I stand and drag her a few feet away to give them privacy. From off in the distance, I realize we're being watched. Logan has stopped at Pete's booth, a cup of coffee in hand, and the two stare our way.

As I guide Lia down the steps, grabbing the empty carrier, Olivia appears once again. "There's a light," she says.

She doesn't seem happy about it. "I feel like...I need to go into it."

"Well, that's a relief," I blurt before I think twice.

Lia gives me a questioning glance. "What?"

I shake my head at her. "Ghost stuff."

Her eyes bug out. "Right here? Right now?" She eagerly searches for the phantom, dropping her cup.

Sage has used one of her pretty china ones rather than the paper kind she hands out to customers. I catch it before it hits the riser. "Olivia, that light is meant for you. Go into it. You'll still be connected to your family, I promise."

"I'm not ready. I haven't said goodbye."

Logan leaves Pete and heads our way. "I'm happy to pass on your message," I assure Olivia. "I can tell them anything you want."

She issues a small sob and vanishes.

"Fudge sticks," I say.

"What happened?" Lia whispers.

I lead her down the rest of the steps, meeting Logan at the bottom. "Doesn't look like they're heading back to the church," he says, tipping his head at our couple.

I accept the coffee he hands me. Brian is walking away, and Tessy is dabbing at her eyes. It's a rough scene to watch, but I suspect it's for the best.

Sipping my drink, I let the warm caffeine soothe my nerves. "Everything's going to work out." I still need to ask Tessy about the man in the black hat. The present moment doesn't seem opportune. "What were you talking to Pete about?"

"He was asking what Tessy was doing here."

"Is that so?" Hmm.

The bleachers vibrate as my bride navigates down the steps, her train flowing behind her. "About those tea leaves? Do you think that Sage would read mine?"

Lia grabs her hand, a big smile on her face. "Of course! You're gonna love her. She's so good at what she does."

As she tugs Tessy behind her, Logan and I follow. When the four of us pass by, Pete calls out, "Hey, Tessy, what are you doing here? Aren't you supposed to be getting married?"

She grins. "I changed my mind." To us, she says, "I think I'm going to be saying that a lot in the coming days."

Pete returns the smile. "Brian was lucky enough to land you once, but you can do better." He winks.

She blushes. "Don't be cheeky."

One of Pete's girls dashes out from behind the table and throws her arms around Tessy's waist. "Hi, Ms. Borage. You look beautiful!"

She pats the girl's back. "Why, thank you. Unfortunately, this dress is going back in storage." It's the original she wore when she walked down the aisle the first time. She looks down at herself and seems to make a decision. "On second thought, maybe I need to burn it. Seems like it's time for me to move on from the past."

"No burning dresses!" I grab my heart dramatically. "That's sacrilege." Everyone chuckles. "If you're agreeable, I'll buy it from you and upcycle it."

Lia nods. "We have a new program where we take vintage dresses, and Gloria remakes them into completely new designs. I bet she could do something *amazing* with yours."

"Sounds like you *and* the dress are getting a fresh start," Pete says.

Tessy nods. "That's exactly what I need."

We continue to Sage's, and Lia recommends the lavender and vanilla white tea blend. I pull Tessy aside while Sage pours the water over the leaves into another of her delicate china cups. "The man you were speaking with earlier? The one with the black hat. Who is he?"

"Uncle Elias?"

"He's your uncle?"

"Oh, no, we're not related. That's what kids called him at school. He was a history teacher at St. Andrew's when I attended the academy. Everyone loved him, and while we addressed him in public as Professor Glassen, we called him 'uncle' behind his back. That's what he was like—a doting uncle who encouraged us. After I graduated, he left under mysterious circumstances. I don't know what happened, but I heard he got mixed up with a..." She screws up her face and lowers her voice. "A witch. He became a total recluse, and folks say she cursed him so he would never leave her."

Lovely. "You don't happen to know this woman's name, do you?"

She thinks about it for a moment. "Haberdash? Hammersmith? Something like that."

"Haversham?"

She snaps her fingers. "That's it! Edie Haversham. I hadn't realized she was a witch! Can you imagine?"s

Sage quirks a brow at me as she hands Tessy her tea. The chaplet is now around her wrist, and she blows carefully on the steaming liquid. "Take your time and concentrate on what you want to ask the leaves," Sage instructs. "When you're finished, I'll read them for the answer."

Tessy stares into the cup and nods. "I know exactly what I want to ask."

So do I, I think, glancing back at Pete. He's watching her with a soft smile on his lips. *So do I.*

And I don't need tea leaves to tell me what the answer will be.

TWELVE

While Tessy sips her beverage, delighted at the flavor, Lia tells her about her internship with me and her ghost hunting with Travis and Wrenlee. She shows her a social media video of theirs that's received over a thousand likes.

Her former teacher seems both amused and slightly horrified. "Ghost hunting? That seems a little...out there, don't you think? Surely, with all the extracurriculars in high school, you could find something more appropriate for a girl your age."

My young friend laughs and slaps her thigh. "*This* is what I love. There's so much about the invisible world we don't realize."

Tessy gives me a questioning look, and I shrug. "Keeps her out of trouble."

Sort of.

"I better get back to the gate and help Travis," Logan

says. "Do you need me to be on the lookout for this Elias guy?"

"Why?" Tessy asks.

I draw Logan away from the table. "I fell yesterday, and he helped me up. I want to thank him." When Lia starts showing her another video, I lower my voice to my husband. "If you see him, let me know and keep an eye on him. We think he may have stolen the necklace and other items."

"Should we call Detective Jones?"

"I'll update Daddy as soon as I can and let him pass it on to Jones. The less I talk to that man, the better."

Logan glances at Kit's booth, where a line of ladies are waiting for readings. "Do you think he took the crystal ball?"

"I haven't been able to place him on this end of the field yet, and I don't want to spook him if he's still around, but I need to ask him a few questions before Detective Jones does."

"I'll keep my eyes peeled." He smiles at me. "I know things haven't gone exactly the way you anticipated, but the market is a hit. I bet we've had twice the number of people today and nearly sold out of all the tote bags. We're running low on maps, too."

If only the ghosts could cross on their own, and I could retrieve my aunt's crystal ball. "Thanks. It's been a joint effort. I couldn't have done any of this without everyone's help, especially yours. I'll text Baylor to bring more maps."

He kisses me before taking off for the gate.

I leave Tessy and Lia with Sage to make my way past Kit's. Joe lets me know he has my soap ready, and I promise I'll be back for it before the end of the day. I'm looking forward to a long, hot bath and his soap.

Kit is busy advising a woman with a tarot reading. I can see by the woman's expression that she's not too happy about what the cards have to say. Kit, being a wise woman, offers support and perspective on the meaning of the sequence she's laid out. I approach Delinda, our masseuse, who vigorously rubs hand lotion into her palms. She's open and friendly and gives me a big smile. "Ava! Did you come for a free massage?"

She was so happy to be included in our event that she promised me a sample of her services. "How about I take you up on it next week? I don't want to take away a slot from a paying customer, and I'm afraid I'm up to my eyeballs in work."

"Let me get my appointment book, and we'll schedule something." She rummages through one of her large bags and withdraws a colorful spiral-bound notebook. "Now that I'm settled in my new place, I'm moving all of my appointments to my digital calendar, but I brought my trusty old manual one for this event."

As she thumbs through the pages to find the one she wants, I'm grateful no one is waiting for her chair. "Have you been busy?"

"It's been great. I have to limit how many I do at once, or my hands and wrists rebel. Even though I'm sticking to that, I guarantee I'll have to plunge these babies into an ice bath tonight." She holds up her hands and wiggles her fingers. "I scheduled two fifteen-minute upper body massages per hour, and I'm booked all afternoon. I've already filled six appointments for this month, too. Once folks get to know where I am downtown, I expect I'll have plenty of clients to pay my rent."

"My friend, Sage, makes an excellent pain cream. It has comfrey and other herbs in it. Talk to her and see if you can get a sample to try. I bet it will help."

"She's the tea gal, right?"

"That's her. Just a couple stalls down from you."

She grabs a pen from her table. "This town has a lot of amazing folks in it. Now, I have Thursday morning at eight or next Saturday at two. Do either of those work for you?"

We settle on the Thursday morning appointment, and I'm already looking forward to it. "With my event planning service, I often offer additional perks. For example, we hire actors to dress up as their favorite cartoon characters or comic heroes when we do kids' birthdays. My brides like spa days. Since we want to be as full-service as possible, I think some of our clients would enjoy including massages. Next month, we have a group of bridesmaids coming in from out of town, and they're staying at the B&B next door to me. What would you think about participating in their girls' night? The Beehive Salon is providing mani-pedis for each of them right there at the B&B. You could offer upper body massages."

Like any good businesswoman, she thinks it over. I can see her running calculations in her head. "How many?"

"Five."

"I could space them out over several hours. How do you handle payment?"

"Since this is a new venture for both of us, we can discuss a flat fee that I'll include in the package price. Going forward, we can negotiate based on the number of people, hours necessary, or whatever you deem fair."

She checks her watch and scans the crowd. It must be

getting close to time for her next appointment. "I like the idea, and I'm definitely interested. Can we hammer out the details on Thursday?"

"Works for me."

"I'll plug this into my software when I get back to the office, and you'll receive a notification and reminder via text."

"Perfect. Can I ask you a question?"

She makes a note on her calendar. "Shoot."

"Did you happen to notice a man in a black hat and trench coat hanging around here yesterday?"

She closes the notebook and sticks it in her bag. "You mean the guy who fell on the table when the mouse ran through?"

"What mouse?"

"Someone yelled 'mouse,' and everyone in line to see Kit started screaming and pushing. This orange cat was hanging around, and it went streaking through, probably chasing that thing." She gives a visible shudder. "I know I jumped on my chair. I don't like mice."

"And the man fell on the table?"

"Sure did. Those ladies in line meant business, shoving people out of the way like a zombie was after them. He must've gotten caught up in the melee and lost his footing."

Had Tabby actually been chasing a mouse? "Do you know who saw this mouse?"

She shrugs as an older man approaches. "I have no idea. Hello, Mr. Carson. Are you ready for your massage?"

I move aside for him. "If you see the man again, will you text me?"

She leads her customer to the chair and helps him get

comfortable. "He was here a little while ago. If he comes back, I'll let you know."

I thank her and walk away.

Before I get to the gate, Persephone intercepts me. "There's trouble in the flea market. You better get over there."

"What kind of trouble? Is Elias back?"

"It's not him. It's Edith. "

She zooms off, passing right through several groups of people enjoying lunch at the picnic tables near the food trucks. Sighing, I have no choice but to follow.

When I arrive, I realize she's right. Edith is tipping over tables, blowing down signs, and sending folks scattering. Like a mini tornado, she seems to be angrier than ever.

"What's going on?" A vendor shouts at me from across the way.

Another calls, "Is this one of those sheer line winds?"

I nod. "Must be." It's not out of the question. We do get them sometimes.

"You have to cross her before she hurts someone," Persephone orders.

"Then help me tame her long enough to do it!"

She rolls her eyes. "Do I have to do everything?"

With everyone trying to hold onto their stuff and shoppers fleeing the area, I don't worry about them witnessing me talking to myself. "This is why I don't want to be a ghost whisperer anymore. I'm so tired of these cranky, ill-mannered spirits. Can you find someone else to do this job?"

She gives me an exasperated glare. "Plenty of people would love to have your gift."

"Name one."

"Ophelia Chen."

She has me there. "She's too young and inexperienced. She thinks it would be fun, but if she knew the reality of this, she'd change her mind in a heartbeat."

"Maybe, maybe not. She'd certainly be a lot easier to work with." She nods as if this idea is growing on her. "In fact, let me see what I can do about that. Then you won't need a guardian angel, and I believe you threatened to replace me earlier, so..."

The 'gift' has been passed down through many generations of my family, skipping most and lying latent in others. Mine wasn't fully activated until after I died, and Logan brought me back to life.

Since I doubt any such gift runs in Lia's genetics, the only way for her to become a ghost whisperer is to experience a near-death event. "Don't you even think about it. You leave that girl alone."

She raises her brows and gives me a slight smile. "If you want to protect her, then stop trying to deny who and what you are. Go deal with that ghost. Now."

If we weren't in public, I would probably give her a rude gesture. She vanishes, and I silently fume.

"Edith." I trail after the gray phantom. "Talk to me. What's got you so upset now?"

"I tried to talk to him! He can't see or hear me."

"Who? Elias?"

"He always said that no matter which of us died first, we could find a way to connect with the other. I'm trying, but he's not listening!"

She's running out of steam. Even with all the living energy here to draw on, she can't sustain enough to keep up her rampage.

She's done a lot of damage, however. As the wind dies and the sellers begin to clean up the mess, she becomes more translucent. She pulls at her own hair. "I hate it here. I hate people. I hate him."

While she may not have been the nicest person during her lifetime, this is what I was explaining to Pete. It's hard to make people understand, but I've seen it time and time again. Many earthbound spirits need closure about their death or something they didn't complete prior to it. Others hang on because of their love for those left behind. In her case, I thought it was her possessions keeping her here, but now I realize that just like Pete and Olivia, Edith is hanging on out of love.

"I'm going to track down Elias, and when I do, you and I will give him your message, okay?"

Her relief is visible on her face right before she disappears.

"Who are you talking to?" the nearest vendor calls to me.

"Nobody," I reply, waving him off.

And once again, I've lost my coffee.

THIRTEEN

A s they march across the field, Daddy and Detective Jones make quite a pair. Jones looks like a linebacker who would be right at home on the turf. Daddy is an aging rockstar. Although he's a former law enforcement officer, he's less bulky and would be a better running back.

The two of them were close when he was on the force, and they still get together occasionally to play poker and smoke cigars. As they approach, Daddy is all smiles, waving his hands as he talks, while Jones is a thundercloud. Even when he's not in the middle of an investigation, he acts as if the entire world is his responsibility to keep in line.

"Hi, sweetie." Daddy kisses my cheek and pats my shoulder. "This place is a zoo. We had to park three blocks down."

People flow around us, some speaking to him, me, and even the detective. Daddy and I happily return the greetings while Jones looks constipated at having to be friendly.

"Has anything else gone missing?" he asks.

"Nothing. So far, so good. I'm happy with how things have gone outside of the thefts. Once you arrest our suspect and return the stolen goods, I can call it a successful event."

I paste on a smile. He doesn't entirely hide an eye roll. "I looked into the name you gave me. Elias Glassen lives in Albertson. No priors. Not even a parking ticket. Why would he drive here and steal a necklace and a puzzle box?"

"That's only ten miles from us. Some folks have traveled farther than that to come to see this. Maybe you should call and ask him that question."

"I already did. He denies any involvement."

Big surprise. "Did he tell you that he was romantically involved with Edith Haversham?"

Jones gives me a blank look. "He admitted they were friends."

"They were more than friends, Detective, which may be why he took those items. I also believe he may have stolen Aunt Willa's crystal ball." I relate the mouse story and how Delinda saw Elias fall on Kit's table. "You should pay him a visit and check out his house. I don't think he plans to resell the stolen goods. He's keeping them for himself."

Jones rocks back on his heels. The overhead sun, now bright in the sky above us, reflects off his bald head. "Schooling me on how to do my job again, Fantome?"

Daddy presses his lips together to hide a grin. "You know the way the law works, Ava. Landon can show up on the man's doorstep, but without a warrant, he can't search the house."

"And there isn't enough evidence to get a warrant," Jones adds.

"So get yourself invited in and do some old-fashioned snooping," I say.

The detective puts his beefy hands on his hips, causing his leather belt to creak. "I've been doing this job a long time. I know how to handle an amateur thief."

"I can see that. You're doing a bang-up job so far."

"Ava," Daddy chastises. "Where are your manners?"

Even though I'm a grown woman, his admonishment makes me feel bad. In all honesty, I think Jones enjoys these sparring matches. He's not offended one bit. "How many thefts do we have in Thornhollow every year?" I ask.

He puffs out his chest. "Last year, we had eight, and I caught every one of the culprits."

Okay, maybe he *is* good at his job. "That's commendable. It instills confidence in me that you'll catch this one."

Agnes Kepler, whose hydroponics farm is three miles outside of town, calls to me from her booth, which is next to Pete's. "Ava? Can I speak to you for a moment?"

"If you'll excuse me, I have a market to run," I say to the two of them. "Daddy, I'll see you later."

Jones calls after me. "Stay out of my investigation, Fantome."

I gave him a thumbs-up and swing over to Agnes' stall. She's a middle-aged woman who runs her place with her brother and son. Her eyes dance and she's smiling from ear to ear. "Sweet Peach Farms just approached me. You know, the one near Gainesville? Their CEO is looking to invest in alternative farming methods, and they're coming to my place next week to have a tour."

"That's wonderful."

She sweeps a hand at her display. Most of her organic

produce has sold out, and she's already put a bunch of empty buckets onto a rolling cart. "An investor could help us expand, and I could start the Little Sprouts Club I've been dreaming of. We need to get kids excited about raising food, don't you think?"

"Absolutely. It's very exciting," I say. "Is there something I can help with?"

"Actually, I was hoping to borrow your husband. I'm not good with contracts and legal jargon, and if they make any kind of offer, I'll need someone like Logan to ensure we protect our assets."

"I'm sure he'd be happy to help." I notice Tessy has returned to Pete's booth and is standing in the U-shape made by the three tables. The girls have left them, probably to get something at the food trucks. I wish I could eavesdrop on their conversation, but there is too much crowd noise. "I'll have him stop by before the day ends to set up a meeting."

She gives me a relieved smile. "Thank you. Cross your fingers that this works out for us. It could open so many doors. We could set up a scholarship program along with the Little Sprouts and who knows what else."

"You're an asset to our community." I tap my clipboard. "I'm starting a list of vendors who want to be included in next year's market. I think with the success of this inaugural kickoff, we can convince the Chamber and City Council to make it an annual event. Would you like me to put you down for a booth?"

"I don't know what the next year will bring for us, but we would be delighted to be included."

I flip a page over and mark her name on the list I've started. "Perfect."

Tessy is gone by the time I head for the gate, leaving Pete with a smile on his face. The girls have returned with food and the three of them eat and laugh in between waiting on customers.

Travis and Logan are happy to see me when I arrive. "We've run out of maps," Logan tells me.

"Baylor is on the way with some."

She comes running through the opening at that moment, holding up a stack in one hand and waving it. "I'm here. I've brought them. Flyers, too. I couldn't find any more totes, though. We'll be sure to order more for next year." She slaps them down on the table. "Sorry, I'm late. I was trying to barcode and enter all the new books I bought yesterday into our system, but the computer kept crashing, and then the barcode printer ran out of ink." She laughs, high and light, and repositions her market tote strap on her shoulder. "Then there was a big traffic jam in front of the church. Apparently, something happened at the wedding."

I squeeze her arm. Today, she's wearing another cute outfit with ladybugs on it. "I'm glad you made it." Trouble with electronics is a sure sign of ghost interference, and I hope the purchases she made yesterday didn't come with one or more attached to them.

"Well." She rubs her hands together, still a bit out of breath. Rummaging through her tote, she pulls out a small camera. "I need to shoot some publicity photos for the Chamber's website. If we get some good ones, we can also use them to advertise next year's event. But I can take over the table if you need me to."

Wrenlee walks through the gate with her head held up,

eyes darting to Travis. "Travis and I can handle it." She glances at me. "If that's all right with you."

"Are you looking for Lia?" I ask.

"She's around here somewhere," Travis says, peering over the heads of a group of women gathered nearby, who are showing off their purchases to each other.

"We talked," Wrenlee says. "I'm not here for her. She said you were swamped and could use extra volunteers."

Never look a gift horse in the mouth. This is another expression that doesn't make much sense to me. I have no idea what a gift horse is or why looking them in the mouth might cause problems, but I understand the gist of it, anyway. "I can most certainly use the help," I tell her with all sincerity.

"Good." She gives me a chin nod. "We've got this."

I grab a second clipboard and shuffle papers between mine and it, handing it to Baylor. "I've started a list of vendors and flea market sellers who want to be notified for next year's event. Anyone who paid the fee and showed up this year is in good standing, and they will get first dibs on a space next year. While you're walking around and getting pictures, if you could check in with each of them and be sure we have their name, phone number, and email, I would appreciate it. We'll send out the sign-up form sometime in November."

"You're always so organized," Baylor says.

"It's the only way I can handle the event planning and wedding gown design businesses." Not to mention the ghosts.

Except, you really can't organize or dictate to them.

They're as rebellious and chaotic as anything I've ever encountered.

When she heads off, I drag Logan to Agnes' booth, explaining why on the way. "This could be huge for her, but she needs to be sure she covers her backside. It's not just her depending on the success of her farm, it's also her brother and son." I know from town gossip that she has invested every bit of her and her late husband's savings into the hydroponics side of things and still has debt. "And I suspect, since that farm has been in their family for generations, she won't be keen on simply being bought out."

He fishes out one of his cards from his back pocket. "I'll take good care of her."

I leave them to it and spot Mama waving at me as she tries to wind her way through the crowd.

We meet in the middle, and I'm not surprised she's in a linen suit and a hat to keep the sun off her face. At least she's traded in her high heels for sensible flats. "There you are," she says. "I've been looking all over for you."

"Is everything okay?"

"Better than okay." She gives me one of her confident smiles. "I've convinced the school board to provide Detective Jones with the security footage that shows the parking lots and football field from yesterday."

"You're amazing." This is excellent news, and combined with the fact he knows we're looking for Elias and his black hat and trench coat, he should have no trouble spotting him and figuring out if he stole the items. "I don't know how you did it, but I sure appreciate it. Maybe I can get Willa's crystal ball back."

She holds up a finger. I've seen that gesture many times growing up. "Nobody messes with my family or my town. We'll catch our thief, and then he'll have to deal with me."

I almost feel sorry for him.

FOURTEEN

The rest of the afternoon goes surprisingly well. Most of the vendors are sold out before closing. Some pack up their tables and tents and visit the ones left. Kit, Sage, and Delinda all still have lines of customers at closing time. Several other service vendors do as well. I grant permission for them to continue selling while the others clean up.

Baylor takes fantastic photos of our sellers and groups of folks shopping, eating, and enjoying themselves. In between my fluttering around like a butterfly, I see her snapping a few of me. I hope she gets my good side.

We have a list of a hundred sellers who want to be notified for the next market. Another sixteen who weren't part of this one but who came by to see it, ask me for information and any forms they need to fill out to secure a spot.

Three food truck owners from nearby towns also approach me, and I have several texts and voice messages from crafters, farmers, and antique dealers who are also interested.

I add all of them to the list, contemplating a larger venue space. The football field isn't going to hold everyone.

Even with the thefts, I consider it a success. Baylor and I will meet with the Chamber members in the following weeks to review what worked and what didn't.

Mama catches up with me while I take a much-needed break on the bleachers. The late afternoon sun bathes the field in a warm glow and the temperature has risen. She's in a lightweight silk tank top and linen slacks. She brushes off the metal before sitting next to me. "We should do a fall event rather than waiting until next spring."

Looking out over the field, which is slowly emptying out, I contemplate it. August is back to school time. She's kicking off a new annual peanut festival in September. Logan's parents always hold a harvest event in October at their vineyard after the grapes have been picked, pressed, and bottled. "I'm not sure how we could do it without interfering with the other celebrations during that time."

"It should coincide with the peanut festival. The collaboration could benefit both of us, and we can share resources when it comes to marketing and promo."

My mother. She thinks of everything.

"You're sure?"

She pats my leg. "You let me worry about the logistics for now. I want a full report on the market next week, and then we'll strategize."

"We can figure out where to dig that pond."

It takes her a moment to recall her expression from yesterday. She chuckles. "Forget the pond. We're building an entire lake. Maybe an ocean." Her gaze looks off into the distance, and I can see the wheels turning in her head. When she glances over at me, she's back to the here and now. "Walker called about an article his nephew is supposed to be writing for the paper. Said you chased him off?"

"Yes, ma'am, I did." I give her the lowdown on my interaction with him. "I haven't had a chance to follow up with Mr. Lee. It's on my list. I'm afraid his nephew was more intent on sensationalizing the larceny than a human interest piece about our success."

The wheels in her head are turning again, this time in a different direction. "He needs to remain unbiased with his newspaper, and I support him in doing so. The paper doesn't come out until Wednesday, so let's hope Landon and your daddy have caught the culprit before the midnight deadline on Tuesday. That way, we can spin the piece in a positive way and give the police department some kudos as well."

She winks before leaving me, engaging several lingering groups on the field. She is always in her heyday when strategizing or hanging out with her constituents. She really does love being mayor, and she's good at it.

My thoughts whirl, and I use my voice memo app to keep track of my ideas. When the well runs dry, I help the booth owners and flea market sellers gather their remaining items and tables and haul them to their vehicles.

No one has seen Elias, and I'm somewhat relieved that I haven't spotted Edith either. Tabby has darted in and out, and I wonder what she's up to. There is no sign of Persephone, but as I'm handing over the keys to the gate to the high school janitor, I notice her boyfriend, Sherlock—named after the famous detective—waving at me from the school's plastic mascot.

A dozen folks are still filing around, and I need to tell Sage, Kit, and Delinda to close up. Lia asks if there's anything else I need from her. Wrenlee and Travis are with her, and the trio seems to be walking on eggshells with each other. At least they're together. "We need to round up our stragglers. Can you politely walk them out?"

She gives me a mock salute. "We're on it."

The three of them bound away. Mama is with Queenie at the food truck, helping her close her windows, shut off the generator, and carefully drive the vehicle off the field. She's the last to exit the back gate, slowly and carefully, waving at me through the window as she goes. I wave back and then motion for Sherlock to meet me under the bleachers so we have some privacy.

"I heard you had quite a weekend," he says, adjusting his round spectacles. "Sorry I've been MIA."

"I know Persephone mandated you stay away since I wasn't cooperating."

"She's a bossy one, and we had a lot of fights over it."

Fights he must have lost. "She's lifted the band, I take it."

A bob of his head. "Said you were back in the game. I must admit, it's good to hear." As usual, he's dressed in a tailored suit with a vest and hat. "I'm allowed to help you with your investigation if you still need it."

"I think we've determined who stole the necklace, pencil box, and potions book. I'm unsure about my aunt's crystal ball, however. I can't find any real connection between it and the other items or it and the now-dead owner of those items, Edith Haversham. From what I've learned, Willa knew her, but it wasn't a friendly relationship. Evidence suggests that our culprit, Elias Glassen, may have taken it, I just don't know what his motivation is. He and Edith were involved in a romantic, and possibly magical, affair."

"The crystal ball is a powerful amplifier," Sherlock says. "Is it possible this Glassen fellow is trying to connect to Edith's spirit by using it?"

"Anything's possible, but why steal it? He could've just asked Kit to do a reading."

"Perhaps he has questions for Edith that he doesn't want to share with a medium or anyone else. It's too personal."

Like Travis.

"That's as good of a reason as any I can come up with, but couldn't he simply buy his own crystal ball to do that?"

"He may have felt he needed something with a proven track record. I imagine if your aunt used hers on a regular basis, it's a powerful artifact. Even someone not gifted with spirit communication might be able to use it as such." Travis again comes to mind. "Like the way you use your cell. You don't necessarily understand the technology, but you believe in it."

"Persephone warned me," I admit, "and I didn't listen."

He chuckles. "Oh, believe me, I know. She was more than happy to share that tidbit when she gave me the green light to speak to you."

Why am I not surprised? "I appreciate any and all help you can give."

He offers a lopsided grin. "I've been itching for a good mystery, and this certainly fits the bill. Let me see what I can find out from the spirit world."

With that, he disappears, and I feel more confident we'll

unravel the situation. I have to get that crystal ball back, and once I do, it will never leave my house again.

"There you are." Logan catches me as I'm leaving the shadows underneath the bleachers. "Meeting your boyfriend under here?"

It was something many of the high schoolers did back in our day. I wonder if they still do. "Sneaking around isn't my style when it comes to romance." I wink. "But play your cards right, and I'll let you pour me a glass of wine and give me a foot massage later."

"Speaking of, you're beat. Your dad and I can handle the rest of this. Why don't you go home, draw a hot bath, and relax?"

"We need to set up the stage for the bands."

"Travis has friends who are going to help. Your dad and I can handle them."

"I really should stay."

He pivots me around and propels me toward the gate. The few remaining T-shirts are packed into one box, my clipboards are stacked next to them, and there's a bag of good-smelling food next to those. "You've done enough. A good boss knows when to delegate, remember?"

He loads me up with the food, clipboards, and box, and I'm swept up as my friends exit with me. Kit tells him she'll make sure I get home safely, and Sage directs Lia and Wrenlee to carry out their tables and tents, pointing them toward the vehicles lined up in the parking lot. "Don't worry," she tells Logan. "We'll take care of her."

I'm deposited on my front porch a few minutes later. I let myself in, watching Lia and Wrenlee unload Sage's equip-ment across the street. I wave to them before I shut the door, dropping my tote bag and the clipboards onto my desk. The box is deposited in an empty chair, and I take the food to the kitchen. While I'd love to eat now, I stick it in the fridge to save until Logan gets home. I send Queenie a text to thank her for thinking of us.

Moxley greets me with tail wags and kisses, but the cats ignore me, each of them peeking open an eye to see if I'm going to feed them. When they realize it's not on the agenda, they drop back to sleep in their favorite spot in the front window.

Exhausted, I plunk onto the sofa, letting my head fall back and kicking my feet onto the coffee table. Moxley tries to jump up next to me, but with his short legs, he struggles to do so. I help him up, and he collapses with his front paws in my lap. I stroke his ears. "We did it, Mox. It was a great event."

He licks my hand and settles his head on his paws. For several long minutes, I do nothing but breathe. Every muscle aches, and my feet may never recover.

I realize I'm dirty and a bit smelly, and Logan's suggestion about a bath sounds good. I promise myself that glass of wine once I'm done to motivate me enough to get to the bathroom.

I run the water and throw in a few drops of my favorite scented oil from Sage. I forgot the soaps I purchased from Joe, which are still downstairs in my bag, but I don't have the energy to get them.

The wine would be excellent while I soak, but I don't have the energy for that, either. I use my bath pillow and sink into the warm water, inhaling the lovely rose and lemongrass scent. "Ahhh..."

"You have a backlog of spirits waiting for you." I startle, splashing water over the edge, my bath pillow falling into the water behind me as I sit up. Persephone lounges on the edge of the vanity. "Monday, we'll have to tackle them."

"Personal space," I yell. "Privacy!"

With no care over my anger, she glances at my naked body as I cross my arms over my chest and bring my knees up to shield myself. "It's not like I haven't seen it before. Why do humans always make such a big deal out of nudity?"

"I'm trying to relax! You are the least relaxing thing I can think of. Get out."

"I let you have Sherlock."

As if this makes it all right for her to drop in unannounced when I'm in the tub? "You shouldn't have ordered him to stay away in the first place. He's my friend."

"He's a ghost. And when you weren't doing your job, it's not like you needed his help."

Reaching for the towel, I strain my arm in order to keep myself covered. It's a fruitless attempt. I'll need to stand if I'm going to grab it. "And you're a guardian angel," I remind her. "You're supposed to help me, not hold me hostage because I won't do what you want. I had a good reason for going on strike, and you know it."

Since she can make herself corporeal, she grabs the towel and hands it to me. "You can't protect your friends from everything. Now, get dressed so we can discuss the other spirits."

I snatch the towel. "You said we'd tackle them Monday. I'm tired, and I helped the ones at the market today, so leave me alone for now. I haven't even had dinner yet."

She starts to reply, then stops and looks toward the door,

cocking her head as if she's listening to something. As I wrap the towel around me and step out of the tub, I hear it, too.

Someone's knocking on my front door. "You might want to get that," she says, walking right through the wall and disappearing.

"Great," I grumble. It's probably Sage or the girls. I dry off quickly and put on my robe. As I step onto the top landing, the knock comes again, harder this time.

It must be someone besides my friends. There's no peephole, but the windows allow me to see most of the porch and street. There's a truck next to my car, but when I lean around Arthur and Lancelot to peek out, I can't tell who it is.

Sage installed a security camera last year, and Lia keeps track of the recordings for me. I've grown warier after certain encounters in my house with those who wish me ill. I tap a couple of keys on my computer, and several views of the porch and yard pop up.

A tall man in a black hat and trench coat raises his hand to beat on the door again. I fish my phone out of my bag and text Logan, Daddy, and Sage. *I've got company, and it looks like it's Elias Glassen.*

While I have no intention of letting that man in, I also don't want him to get away. Sage will come running any second after she gets my text. I wrap my robe tighter and slip on a pair of shoes tucked under the coat rack before I crack open the door. "Hello, Elias," I say.

He looks at me with steady eyes, unsurprised I know his name. "A little bird told me you were looking for me. What can I do for you, Mrs. Cross?"

"Have a seat in one of the rocking chairs, and I'll be right with you," I tell him.

He looks like he's going to disagree but thinks better of it. "Fine."

I close the door and consider what I have on hand to use as a weapon, just in case. A pair of scissors, a baseball bat Logan keeps in the corner, my small stun gun.

I don't want to hurt the man; I only want answers, but I'm too on edge and jaded these days not to be prepared.

I make sure the cameras are recording him while I grab the stun gun and slide it into my robe pocket. Help is on the way, and I feel better being prepared if he does anything to threaten me.

Confident I will get to the bottom of this, I paste on a smile and join him on the porch.

FIFTEEN

I see no activity across the street and wonder if Sage is too busy to notice her phone. Tabby appears on her front steps, tail flicking. Meeting my gaze, she goes to one of the outdoor tables and flops down on it as if she's going to watch the show. Why is she staying over there?

You better watch out for that one, the door knocker advises.

I don't trust him, gargoyle number one says.

He's powerful, though, his companion adds.

If help won't come to me, maybe I need to go to it. Elias hasn't sat in the chair but paces along the railing. I don't feel comfortable sitting if he's not.

You're all alone, the door knocker warms.

She was never too bright, gargoyle number one states.

Oh, for heaven's sake. If only to get away from them, I gesture at the teahouse. The sun has dipped behind the houses the street over, shadows rising as the temperature begins to cool. "I could use something to drink. Why don't we walk to Tea Leaves and discuss this?"

I don't wait for his reply and start down the steps. Yes, I'm dressed in only my robe, but Sage isn't officially open. Hopefully, none of the neighbors notice me traipsing about like this, but I'd rather risk that gossip than end up in a dire situation.

I don't hear Elias following, but I keep going. Either he'll come along or jump in his truck and drive off. He came here for a purpose, and if he is our thief, he's going to try and throw suspicion on someone else.

For a big guy, he moves stealthily, and I nearly jump when he says, "Seems like you recovered from your fall yesterday quite well. Do you always walk about in your robe?"

He's right behind me. I don't look back, passing through the open gate at the end of the sidewalk and scanning the front windows of the tea shop. "I'm fine, and no, I don't. Today is an exception."

No one's in the cul-de-sac, and I cross the street with my head held high.

"That place is closed," Elias says.

"I'm friends with the owner. She'll open for us."

He stops at the bottom of the stairs, eyeing Tabby, who watches us closely with narrowed, golden eyes. "I don't drink tea. Just tell me what you want."

I ease into the chair at the table where Tabby lies. "Tell me about the mouse."

His brows draw together, and he thunks a heavy foot on the bottom step. "What mouse?"

"You were at Kit's booth yesterday, and from what I heard, someone shouted about a mouse, causing panic."

Nothing changes in his body language, but I see something flicker behind his eyes. "I never saw it. There was some shoving and screaming. What of it?"

"Did you steal my aunt's crystal ball?"

He laughs as if I'm as loony as I look. "Why in the blue blazes would I do that? I've got no use for such a thing."

Sage runs out the door, stopping short when she sees us. Her phone is in her hand, and she looks slightly relieved to see me, then perplexed at my attire. Her face morphs again as she realizes Elias is blocking me in. "Oh," she says, shifting easily into an impersonal manner. "I didn't realize I had customers."

"What's going on here?" Elias's eyes go hard and dart between us. "What do you really want, Mrs. Cross? I drove all the way over here to answer your questions, and now you're acting as goofy as your aunt used to."

"You knew Aunt Willa?"

He places a hand on the banister, a casual gesture. "I had no reason to know her well."

"So you *didn't* know her?"

"What's this got to do with anything?"

He seems truly confused. Sage and I exchange a glance,. "Why don't you have a seat, and I'll bring tea?" she offers. "You look like a pomegranate and spice kind of guy."

He flips his fingers dismissively. "Like I told her, I don't drink the stuff, and this is wasting my time."

I need a different tactic. "I understand you were close to Edith Haversham."

The previous casualness slips a bit. His fingers tighten on the banister. "What about her?"

"A few of her things went missing from the flea market. We're trying to find out who took them. Do you have any ideas?"

His knuckles turn white as his grip tightens. "Her grand-daughter shouldn't be selling her things. There are people who want them as keepsakes, even if Sadie doesn't."

"Like you?"

Tabby raises herself, arching her back in a stretch before she sits, wrapping her tail around her.

"What's with her?" he asks instead of answering my question.

I stroke her back, which she dislikes, but I swear her mouth curves in a wicked grin. "Answer the question. Do you have any idea who would steal Edith's belongings?"

He pushes away from the steps. "You accusing me of something, girl?"

I stand, and even though I'm on the landing, I'm barely taller than him. "I realize this may have escaped your notice, but referring to me as a girl is derogatory. I'm a grown woman and your equal. You were involved with Edith Haversham, and some of her things have gone missing. If you stole them—"

"*Stole* them!" He gives a disgusted grunt. "That's what you want? To accuse me of being a thief?"

Sage and Tabby watch the exchange with wariness, ready to defend me. I sure hope, with the backlight of the shop's window behind me, I'm not putting more on display than is proper. Ironic that I am confronting this man about Edith in similar attire to hers. "I'm trying to get to the bottom of this, and I thought you might have an idea about who would do such a thing. I haven't accused you of anything other than being her friend. Do you want to help me get to the bottom of this or not?"

He seems to reconsider his bluster. If he's guilty, this gives him a way into my snooping to try and control it. If he's innocent, he should want to help. "I can't think of anyone off the top of my head. If I do, I'll let you know." He tips his hat to us and walks away.

I scramble down the stairs and follow him to his truck. My fingers graze the stun gun in my pocket, and I consider accidentally hitting him with a jolt to keep him from leaving. He's about to run if he is guilty, and we'll never catch him.

But I feel he's not done collecting those pieces of Edith's belongings that are dear to him. Mentally, I call her, asking her to help me figure out what to do. "I'm sorry if I offended you," I tell him. "It's been a stressful weekend, and now that the event is over, I'm afraid I've lost any hope of finding the culprit."

He hesitates at the driver's door. "Maybe you should leave it to the police. They are looking into it, right? That detective already interrogated me as if I were to blame. It seems to me the two of you have already decided I'm guilty."

"We are covering all the bases. Your name has come up several times in connection to Edith." I'm frantically searching for another direction to take this to keep him from leaving before Daddy and Logan get here. Both of them are better at questioning suspects than I am. "Tessy Borage thinks very highly of you. I saw you talking to her today after she ran away from her wedding."

His features soften at her name. "She's one of the good ones," he says. "Deserves better than that jerk Brian."

"You know him?"

"I know he's in love with her, but he's not good for her. She learned that the last time. Seems like she's smartened up."

With that, he gets in his truck and pulls out.

Sage and Tabby wait on the sidewalk in front of the tea house. They've heard everything. "Well, that was unexpected," Sage says.

Wrenlee and Lia emerge from the shop. "I got as much recorded as I could." Lia holds up her phone. "I don't think he gave us anything incriminating, though."

"Why did he come to your house?" Sage asks.

I pulled my robe tighter, watching as Logan, Daddy, and Detective Jones all race up to the house. "He said a little birdie told him I was looking for him. Who do you think it was?"

My grandmother meows and slinks off before the men hustle across the street.

Sage lowers her voice. "I could smell it on him, the residue from the bag. It was on his clothes."

"He's been in contact with the crystal ball?"

She nods. "Definitely."

"So he did steal it."

"Most likely." She taps her phone screen. "I'm going to try that locator spell again."

"Ava?" Logan takes the stairs in one leap. "Are you okay?"

I reassure him I am. "Just an unexpected visitor."

"What happened?" Daddy asks.

Jones glances around. "Where did he go?"

I fill them in on the encounter, and Lia shares the somewhat muted voice recording she's captured. The last part of our conversation she couldn't get due to the distance, but I give them the gist of it.

"Way to go, Fantome," Jones says, frustration in every word. "You've chased off our one and only lead."

"What was I supposed to do? He showed up on my doorstep, and I wasn't going to blow the opportunity to ask him what he knew about the missing items."

"You should have alerted me and waited until I got here."

"He'd already be gone. Look, I tried to detain him as long as I could."

Daddy pats my back. "Logan, take her home. She's had a rough couple of days. Landon and I will figure this out."

Daddy motions for Jones to follow him across the street. Once they're at the police cruiser, Logan gives me a questioning look. "Did you tell him everything?"

"I did," I admit. "Everything except the fact that I don't think a little birdie told him anything. He's got the crystal ball. That's how he knew."

Sage nods. "It's possible he heard through the grapevine that Ava wanted to talk to him, but it's more likely he was messing around with that and learned she was onto him."

"You think he came here to do her harm?" Logan asks.

"Good thing we were here." Lia rests an arm around Wrenlee's shoulders. "We weren't about to let anything happen to our favorite ghost whisper, were we?"

Wrenlee crosses her arms and lifts her chin in defiance. "No way. We had her back."

Logan gives each of them a brief smile, then returns his focus to Sage.

She shrugs. "Attacking Ava has no purpose since she has no proof. He probably just wanted to see how much she knew."

"Standing right here," I remind them. "Of course, he wanted to know how much I had figured out." Unfortunately, now he knew. What would he do with that information? "I want to go to his house tonight. Do some snooping."

A resounding chorus of "no" makes me take a step back. The police cruiser is pulling out, and Daddy waves from his car before trailing the detective down the street.

"Your dad and Jones are dealing with it," Logan insists. "Your only job tonight is to get some rest."

Against my better judgment, I allow him to lead me home. I have the feeling this isn't over between me and Elias Glassen.

SIXTEEN

Sunday morning after church, Pete Younkers catches me in the parking lot. "Hate to bother you." He nods at Logan. "I was wondering if I could speak to Ava for a moment."

Last night, I told my husband all about him, Tessy, Edith, and Sadie. How Persephone blackmailed me into helping the ghost, and how I had to help the living as well. Logan had just squeezed my shoulder with a smile. "It's good to have you back. All of you."

"You're not upset?" I'd asked him.

"I know you want to keep everyone safe, but this is who you are, Ava. Each of us wants to wrap our loved ones in a bubble, but life doesn't work that way. And you've taken precautions—you've set up fail-safes here at the house, you have Sage and Kit teaching Lia how to defend herself from ghosts, and you have powerful friends to offer guidance and watch your back."

I'd stared into my wine and thought about it. Back in the

day when Daddy was on the force, I remembered a period of time after one of the suspects in a case he was investigating had threatened me and Mama. He'd become so wrapped up in guarding us that he'd become paranoid.

It had been a tough few months, but Landon Jones had reminded him of his training and expertise. The detective had done a good thing that day, empowering my dad to believe in himself again and reminding him that he had taught Mama and me how to take care of ourselves.

"There are more things I want to do to safeguard us," and I'm considering this as a test run," I'd argued, "but I don't want to become paranoid and reclusive. I also need to make sure none of you are put in harm's way because of me."

He'd pulled me close, and I'd laid my head on his shoulder. "I know, and I also believe that when our time is up, it's up. There's no sense in taking stupid chances, but on the other hand, odds are, we're both going to live long and healthy lives."

"Because of what Kit told us?"

He chuckled. "Yep, and so far, every prediction she's had has been accurate."

Outside the church, the sun is warm on my face, and when he nods at me to go ahead, I smile at Pete. His daughters are at his vehicle, one texting on her phone, while the younger sits on the tailgate reading a book and swinging her legs. "Does this involve them?" I ask.

We walk away from Logan, who joins my parents even as he keeps an eye on me, and Pete fiddles with his tie. "I laid it all out for them last night. I told them what you had said to me. I thought they'd be freaked out, but they took it pretty well. They both admitted to feeling their mom's presence at different times."

Several people hail us, and we reply with greetings, waiting for them to move on before we resume our conversation. "That's great," I tell him. "Are we still on for Wednesday?"

"Do you think Olivia will be upset with me?"

"About wanting her to move on?" It's a tough call, but after the way she reacted yesterday about Tessy, I believe she might take it easier now. "I think she wants you to be happy."

At that moment, Olivia appears, staring at him. "I never loved anyone but him," she says.

"Pete,"—I smile—"she's here with us."

He jerks a bit and scans the area. "Right now?"

"She wants you to know that she never loved anyone but you."

He swallows a few times. "Tell her that I felt the same way from the moment I saw her."

"She can hear you. You can speak directly to her."

He doesn't know what to do with his hands now and crushes the end of his tie. "Olivia? Are you here?"

The tree branch overhead rustles with a light breeze in answer. "I see that light again," she says to me. "It keeps tugging at my chest."

"That's a good thing," I respond. "That means it's time."

Pete gives me a funny look, and I explain to him what's happening, before I say, "Pete, do you have anything else you want to tell Olivia before she crosses over?"

"So many things," he says, his eyes tearing up. "The girls and I... It's hard to go on without you, Liv."

She offers a wan smile. "Tell him that he needs to. For

them. They need him to be strong, to be happy. That's all I ever wanted for my family."

I relay the message. A tear streams down his cheek. "I'll do my best to care for them and raise them the way you would want."

She looks off toward the distance, and I can see the glow of the afterlife doorway. "Tell him to take care of himself, too. He shouldn't be alone. He's going to need help with the girls, especially Megan. She's as bullheaded as I am."

Once more, I relate her words, and he laughs. "I love you, Liv."

She glances at me. "Tell him I love him, too, and that I'll be back to watch over all of them. Tell him to be nice to Tessy. She'll make a good mom to the girls."

With that, she disappears. The next second, I see her in the doorway, turning back to wave at us before her ghostly form fades into the light.

"She's gone," I tell him, adding her final words and squeezing his shoulder when he breaks down.

After he collects himself, cleaning off his tears with a hanky, he clears his throat. "Thank you. I still can't believe it, but I guess ghosts are real, huh?"

Boy, are they.

"Dad?" Megan calls. "Can we go now? I'm hungry."

He pockets his hanky. "Be there in a minute." To me, he says, "What did she mean about Tessy?"

"There's no timeline when it comes to grief and moving on, but keep an open mind. You have Olivia's blessing if you want to pursue a relationship with her and I don't know how it gets better than that. She seems like a good match for you and your daughters."

That afternoon, I'm still feeling happy about the outcome with him as I check on the first band to make sure the stage is set up to their standards. I stand by while they do a sound check, and Sadie Haversham approaches, looking upset. "Someone broke into my house last night. Can you believe it?"

I draw her away so we don't have to shout over the speakers while the band begins a warm-up. We duck into one of the school doorways. "Are you all right? Did they take anything?"

"I wasn't there. I went to The Thorny Toad for a drink with a friend, and when I returned, the door was wide open."

"You live in Edith's house, right?"

"Just while I'm sorting everything out. There's still so much stuff in that place, there's no way I can tell if anything's gone. She collected everything under the sun. Miniature tea sets, cat figurines, salt and pepper shakers, snow globes." She gives a frustrated sigh. "I haven't even dug into the attic or basement yet. That's why I told you I have to sell some of it. A lot of it. It's like she was one of those hoarders you see on TV or something." A gleam enters her eyes. "Say, I wonder if I contacted one of those reality shows, they'd come and do an episode about her. Do you think they'd pay me?"

Edith bursts in and, even in her ghastly gray form, looks as though she might blow a blood vessel. "Are you kidding me? I can't believe this girl. I blame her mother. She never taught her any values."

"Did you call the police?" I ask Sadie.

"Yeah, I spoke to him." She points, and I follow the direction of her finger to see Detective Jones striding toward us. She raises her voice. "Did you catch the guy?"

"What guy?" I ask.

Jones reaches us, briefly flicking his gaze at me before speaking to her. "Your neighbor's security camera didn't catch his face. Did you inventory everything like I asked?"

"It would take me years to inventory that house," Sadie whines. "Look, if he stole anything, he did me a favor. Unless it's valuable—then I want it back."

I can literally see Jones grinding his teeth. I sympathize. "You caught the thief on video?" I ask. "Was it Elias?"

"Can't tell," Jones says. "Her neighbor has a doorbell camera, and it recorded what appears to be a man entering and leaving the premise along the hedge row."

"Elias? Nah. Whoever it was probably came back for the rest of those books," Sadie says. "It's a good thing they were still in my car. None of that left from yesterday is worth a hoot, though, really. I should just drop it off at Goodwill first thing tomorrow."

Edith shrieks, throwing up her hands. "Do something!" she shouts at me.

"But you're saving that one we talked about, right?" I ask.

Her face brightens. "It's just like you said—Nana had all these notes written in it. I'm saving that for sure."

Edith relaxes a smidgen.

"From now on, lock your doors when you're not there," Jones tells her.

"Yeah, yeah. I know. You don't think he'll come back, do you? Try to kill me or something?"

The detective looks as though he might cheer the guy on if he did. "No." Mentally, I swear I hear him add, *unfortunately*.

"I have to get back to the band," I say, trying to hide my grin. "I'll just leave you two to discuss this."

"Not so fast, Fantome," Jones barks, shifting to block my exit from the nook. "Ms. Haversham and I are done."

His glare sends her scooting off without another word.

I try to edge around him, but he puts his hands on his hips and stops me. "What? Do you think her break-in last night *is* Elias?"

"Most likely, yes. However, he was wearing a hoodie rather than a trench coat and hat. But he knows we've made him in that outfit, so he switched to another to throw us off. Since he was involved with Edith, I'm sure he knew she didn't have any kind of security at the house and that Sadie never locked the door. What do you think he was after?"

"How would I know?"

He tilts his head, challenging me. "You know a lot of things you shouldn't. Maybe you should ask your ghost friends to help."

Edith continues to hover nearby, and I give her a pointed look. She's supposed to be doing precisely that, yet she hasn't done anything. "I'm sure I don't know what you're talking about. If you haven't noticed, I'm running an important community event, and I'm a bit busy."

"I spent the whole night reviewing footage from the school. Guess who I found leaving the market with a big bulge under his coat?"

My pulse kicks up. "Elias? I knew it. He did steal the crystal ball."

"Along with that and the other testimonies, not to mention the suspicion about him breaking into Edith's last night, I have enough to bring him in for questioning."

"What about a search warrant? I need to get in his house and see if he still has it."

His hands return to his hips in that habitual gesture, making him appear even larger than he already is. "Cool your jets. Even if he does, it's evidence, and you can't have it back until he goes to trial."

The band has quit warming up, disappearing behind the stage to prep for their grand entrance. They're kicking off the concert lineup. Lia bounds over to us. "There you are," she says to me. Then she glances at him. "No one says 'cool your jets' anymore, Detective."

He ignores her. "I've reached out to Judge Warner about a warrant, and I'm waiting to hear back, but most of this is still circumstantial and hearsay, so I probably won't get it. That's why I want to bring Glassen in for questioning."

"So do it," I say. "What are you waiting for?"

"I have to track him down. He's not answering his phone, and I spoke to his neighbors, all of whom claim he was in and out several times yesterday and last night. I'm going to Albertson to track him down."

In and out several times? "If he knows we're onto him, he may have loaded up his truck and gone on the run." My earlier excitement turns to disappointment. "I'll never see that crystal ball again."

"Ava." Lia tugs on my arm. "The band is waiting for you to announce them. Do you want me to do it?"

She asks with far too much enthusiasm, but maybe I should let her do it. I certainly don't feel like I can muster the excitement to be a good emcee at this point. "Go ahead." I hand her the three-by-five card on which I've written an introduction. "Use this."

"Really?" She bounces on the balls of her feet. "You're letting me do it?"

"I sure am."

She throws her arms around me in a bear hug, squeals, and then runs to the stage.

Jones shakes his head. "You're not going with me, so don't even ask."

I hadn't thought of it, but now that he said that... "Why not? I can turn the other duties over to someone else and come with you. A stakeout."

"Not by anything that's holy would I go on a stakeout with you. Stay here and do your job while I do mine. I'll let you know if I find Willa's ball."

It's nice that he came to update me. I have to cut him a little slack. "That means a lot to me. Thank you. I mean it."

He eyeballs me, searching for sarcasm. Finding none, he shakes his head and takes off.

Edith vanishes, too, as my young intern grabs the stage mic and begins rousing the crowd into enthusiastic applause for the band.

I leave the nook and make my way to the seat Logan has saved for me, pretending to enjoy the performance as I stew over Elias Glassen. I itch to take things into my own hands.

SEVENTEEN

By the time my father takes the stage for the finale, I'm nearly beside myself. I do his introduction—to Lia's disappointment but to his pleasure.

"Growing up," I tell the audience. We've doubled in size since the first band played. "My father would sing me lullabies to put me to sleep. He'd be out in the garage on his days off from the force, playing his guitar and writing song lyrics. I loved his voice then, and I still do. Our town is lucky that he's returned home, and I'm lucky because he's my father."

Mama hoots, and there's a smattering of applause. I hold my hand out to him, where he stands behind me, and motion him forward. He's been a solo act for a while but has recruited Doria Washburn and Ivan DeLuca to help him today. They take their places at the drum and keyboard.

My smile is genuine as I say, "Everyone, please welcome Nash Fantome and Phantoms."

Cheers and more applause greet him. He kisses my

cheek, strums his guitar, and the first notes of a rock song kick in.

It's easier for me to forget Glassen, Edith, and the rest as I tap my foot and sing along. The Phantoms do the first set of covers, then another of songs Daddy wrote and normally performs on his own. I like the depth the drums and keyboard add to them, but hearing my father sing acapella is still my favorite.

Movement near the stage catches my eye—a switching orange tail disappears around the back of the stage. I'm not the only one who sees it. Kit, seated behind me, leans forward and whispers in my ear. "Is that your grandmother?"

I nod but ignore Tabby.

Kit pokes me. "I think she wants you to follow her."

I glance at the corner of the stage where Tabby disappeared and see her peeking at me. What does she want now?

But I know better than to spurn or disregard her attempts to show me something. I murmur to Logan that I'll be back in a minute, and then I take the long way around the crowd so I don't distract from Daddy.

Behind the audience, I trail by the south side of the parking lot, sneaking behind the central area of the high school's dull mango-colored bricks. The flag isn't flying today, but the parking places are full. I catch sight of Tabby crossing between a couple of SUVs and padding down the sidewalk on a side street.

Tabby glances over her shoulder to see if I'm following. Sherlock appears, waving me forward.

Above, clouds approach from the west. As I try to catch up with them, I check my weather app. Sure enough, the prediction has changed, and a powerful spring system is moving our way.

I offer a prayer that my father is able to finish his concert before it rains. Even as I trot down the sidewalk, calling Tabby's name, the wind picks up. Peony bushes lining a yard bend toward me, and I catch the scent of roses as I pass another.

"This way." Sherlock points. "You have to stop him."

"Elias?"

He nods. "He's got the stolen items! Pretend you're chasing your runaway cat so he doesn't get suspicious."

"Good idea," I say to him, even though Elias will know that's not true if he catches me.

Tabby slips under a van, and I see movement behind it. I slow my pace, edging around to that side of the street and halting under a towering maple.

A man leans through the side door, mumbling to himself as he paws through cardboard boxes. He's stacked three on the ground near his feet, their flaps open and the contents in disarray. There are candlesticks, snow globes, and assorted knickknacks, including cat figurines.

Two cars down, I notice a familiar truck.

Elias Glassen's. I glance skyward, not to check on the approaching storm but to mentally call for Persephone. "Thanks, Sherlock," I whisper, hoping he hears me.

The dumpy van has faded spots on the hood, scratches on the side panels, and a broken rear taillight. Tabby emerges from underneath, sits next to the stacked boxes, and gives me a bored glance before she uses her paw to clean her face.

Quietly, I back up several steps, pulling out my phone from my back pocket. I'm about to text Logan when Elias catches sight of Tabby. "You again." A second later, it dawns on him that wherever the cat is, he sure finds me. His head jerks up.

Our eyes meet, and he swears a blue streak, tossing the box he's rummaging through at my grandmother. She deftly avoids it and the contents when it tips over. "If you know what's good for you," he snarls, "you'll get out of here. Now."

I fire off a 911 to Logan. "Is this Sadie's van? Are you stealing more of Edith's possessions?"

"Stealing them? They belong to me."

"How so? She willed them to Sadie."

He knocks the sweatshirt's hood back, revealing his balding head, and taps his chest with a thumb. "The things I took are ones I gave her. They're mine, and so are a whole lot more."

He glances at another box inside the van, seeming to debate whether he should keep searching for whatever it is he wants or take off. He's not scared of me, nor does he seem worried I'll be able to stop him. He reaches inside to pull the box across the seat and begins flipping items out of it.

"Stop it," I say. "You have no right to any of that."

He bangs a fist on the seat. "She wasn't supposed to die yet."

It's as if he's talking more to himself than to me.

Edith pops in at that moment, watching him with a frown on her face. "What are you doing, old man?"

She's probably the best distraction I have at the moment. "She's here and wants to know what you're doing."

He looks up, startled. Then, thinking this is a joke, he snickers and returns to his sorting. "Nice try. I don't believe in all that garbage about ghosts and mediums."

"You're not the only one," I say to him, then to Edith, "Tell me something only you know about him."

He makes a face at me. "What?"

Tabby meows, angling herself at the back of his leg and extending her claws. I snap my fingers to stop her, and she gives me a rueful look.

Edith examines the boxes on the ground and her spilled belongings. "The snow globe he wants isn't here. It's the Hawaiian one, with sand and a palm tree. There's a shorebird and a hibiscus. Sadie kept it. Can you believe it? That ugly thing?"

She explains why it's important, and I could hug her. "The Hawaiian globe that you gave her," I tell Elias. "It's not in there. It's still in the house, and she claims that you were going to run away together and live in Hawaii. That's why you gave it to her."

He stops digging. "Still in the house? That dimwitted girl. Where'd she hide it?"

Edith tells me, but I'm not about to share the location. "You're a thief, and you need to stop this. Turn yourself in to Detective Jones and let him return the items to their rightful owners."

"I told you," he growls. "I gave her those things. They belong to me. They're important to me, not that dumb granddaughter of hers."

Edith shrugs. "At least he'll appreciate them."

I shake my head. "That's not how it works."

He thinks I'm talking to him and comes at me, fury reddening his face. "Those things are all I have left of her, and you're not taking them from me."

I hold up my hands, considering the heavy iron candlestick two feet away. It's a gaudy thing that looks like a Halloween prop; I bet it weighs as much as Aunt Willa's crystal ball. "There's no reason to get upset. We can talk this out."

"Tell him there's a box of my things in the basement specifically for him. It has his name on it. I want him to have them."

"What things?" I ask.

He screws up his face but stops his approach.

"The nightgown he gave me when I ruined my favorite one. A picture of us at Niagara Falls." She smiles as she reels off a complete inventory, and I cut her off before she's finished. Elias has balled his fists, and I debate whether to run or grab the potential weapon.

"She kept the ticket stubs to the first concert you attended," I say, stepping sideways and snatching up the candlestick. It's indeed heavy and will do the job if I need it.

Elias cocks his head. "What?"

"She created a keepsake box and put your name on it. It has the ticket stubs, the nightgown you gave her, and a picture of you two at Niagara Falls. There's more. Those things are yours, but they're at the house, and you need to ask Sadie to give them to you. Give her back the items you stole in exchange."

His anger is replaced by shock. He stumbles backward, his heel slipping on the edge of the curb. His arms cartwheel to keep him from falling, and he rights himself. "How do you know that?"

I stay where I am. Tabby moseys over to sit at my feet. "Edith told me. Like I said, she's here. Is there anything you want to say to her before she crosses to the afterlife?"

All the color drains from his face, and he lumbers toward his truck.

"He's got the crystal ball," Edith confesses. "You better stop him before he gets away."

From the direction of the school, I hear Logan calling my name. Although he received my urgent message, he doesn't know where I am. "Over here," I yell as loud as I can. I glance at the nearest house number. "Twenty-one twenty-three!"

Tabby hops onto a nearby car's hood and leaps, extending her nails. Spreadeagle, she sinks her claws into his back, and he falls to his knees, screeching in pain.

My phone rings, Logan. I repeat into the phone what I yelled, assuming he couldn't hear me over Daddy's music. "It's Elias Glassen. He's trying to get away. Hurry!"

Elias struggles to his feet, trying to yank Tabby off. She hangs on for dear life, even though he manages to grab one of her rear legs. I kick at the back of his knees, and he goes down again.

Tabby falls and limps away, dragging her leg, but I don't have time to tend to her. In a quick move, Elias shoves me down onto the sidewalk, the candlestick clattering out of my grip. He climbs on top of me, pinning me to the hard concrete, and draws back a meaty fist. "You shouldn't have messed with this. It's none of your business."

I squeeze my eyes shut. "It became my business when you took my aunt's crystal ball!"

The sound of approaching footsteps surprises Elias. "Ava!" Logan yells. "Hey, get off her!"

The man jumps to his feet, kicking me in the ribs, before he dashes to his truck. He yanks open the passenger door, and when he turns, I see the very item that means so much to me in his hands. "You want this?"

He raises the crystal ball above his head, and my heart freezes as I realize his intent. "No!" I scream.

But Elias hurls it through the air, aiming it at the sidewalk.

EIGHTEEN

Logan was a star athlete in school—football, basketball, and even baseball. All these years later, there is something about his natural grace and ability that kicks in.

I roll to my hands and knees to lunge for the crystal ball, but he's already flying through the air like a professional running back with his arms extended.

It's only an inch from smashing into the sidewalk when he latches onto it. His body hits with a hard thump, and I hear a crack as the ball does make contact.

He rolls, tucking it into his belly, and I feel like cheering.

"I can't believe El did that," Edith says, seeming flabbergasted. "What is wrong with him?"

Elias makes a fist, and I cringe as I see it headed for my nose. Before it makes contact, my weapon lifts from the ground and whacks him on his temple.

He staggers, hits, and rebounds off the side of his truck.

Then he does an awkward bellyflop, landing a few feet from Logan.

My husband winces as he springs to his feet. "Here." He lobs the ball at me. I'm not as gifted as he is, but I do catch it, mirroring his hold and clutching it to my belly. He rounds on Elias and stomps his foot onto the man's back, keeping him pinned. "I suggest you stay down."

Elias rolls and grabs Logan's leg. The two brawl but Edith isn't done. With the same magic she used to wallop Elias with the candlestick, she begins pelting him with items from her boxes. A few of them hit Logan, too.

I don't know what to do, glancing between the ball, Sadie's van, and the fighting men. I want to help Logan, so I set the crystal ball in the grass. "Be careful!" I yell at Edith as one of her cat figurines hits Logan in the cheek before it falls to the sidewalk and busts.

I pick up the candlestick and smack Elias on the shoulder. He grunts and pivots, taking a swing at me. I duck, and he misses.

The action costs him, leaving him off balance. When he tries to right himself and fend off Logan, who is advancing on him again, Logan lands an uppercut. Elias goes stiff, wobbles for a heartbeat, and falls to the ground.

Lights out.

Logan holds his arms out to me. I rush into them, breathing hard. "Are you hurt?" he asks.

"No, I'm okay. Thank you for saving the crystal ball."

"It's still broken," Edith says.

I draw back from Logan. I hear a crack and... "Oh, no."

She hovers over the ball on the lawn. "There's a chunk missing."

Sure enough, a small divot has been knocked out, and a fine fissure encircles the sphere.

Logan swears softly under his breath. "If I'd only been a second faster. I'm sorry."

I hug the ball to me and smile into his face. "If it weren't for you, this would be in a thousand broken pieces." And so would my heart. "You saved it, and I'm so grateful."

He rubs my back. "I'll call Detective Jones and let him know what just transpired. I'm sure he'll want your full account."

Edith stands over Elias, shaking her head. "What happened to him? He wasn't like this when I was alive."

Sage and Kit charge up the sidewalk toward us. I hugged the ball a little tighter. "Grief does funny things to people." Logan gives me a curious look. "Edith is here," I explain. "She's the one who hit you with the cat figurine. She's trying to understand why Elias went off the deep end after she died. She claims he wasn't like this before."

He nods and walks a few feet away, pulling out his phone to call Jones.

Kit and Sage reach us, staring at the mess. "What happened?" Sage asks.

Kit grins, pointing at the crystal ball. "You got it back."

I show them the damage and tell them the story. "I don't suppose either of you know how I can fix this?"

Sage rustles through pieces of broken figurines and other items, finding the missing chunk and handing it to me. "It's not good for divination now, but since you never use it for that purpose, dab epoxy on this piece and stick it back in there. Problem solved."

Kit agrees. "It's a keepsake, and your connection to your aunt can never be broken."

I glance at Elias, a deeper understanding of his obsession with Edith's belongings taking hold. Tabby limps out from behind a tree trunk and meows. She's still dragging her back paw. "Oh, Tabitha. Thank you for your help. I'm so sorry you got hurt. Do you need to go to the vet?"

She hisses, showing me her fangs.

Okay, then. "I take that's a no."

Sage strokes her fur, gently probing the injury. "Can you morph back to human?"

Tabby gives her a nod.

"Good," Sage glances at me. "I'll take her to my shop. She'll be back to normal in no time."

"I don't think I want to stay here anymore," Edith says to me. "Everyone's gone mad. Back in the day, Elias would never hurt an animal." She shakes her head with sad eyes as she stares at his prone body. He moans, coming around.

This is my chance. "Do you see a lighted doorway?"

She lifts her gaze and scans the area. "I'm not sure what's waiting for me on the other side. I'm scared."

I could use some help here to ease the transition, guardian angel. "Is there anyone on the other side who might be waiting for you?" I ask Edith. This is a standard line when my ghost is nervous about karma. "A relative? A good friend? A pet?"

Her wary eyes meet mine. Thunder booms in the distance, and I try not to flinch. The wind picks up, and it pastes her nightgown to her body. She crosses her arms and rubs them as if suddenly chilled. "My dad died when I was twenty-one, and I missed him every day. He didn't get to give me away when I got married. But I felt him with me." She gives a small smile. "You think he'll be there? Wherever it is I'm going," she adds.

"I don't know the details about the afterlife," I explain, "but what I do know is that it's peaceful. It offers a chance for your soul to rest, and then you can reconcile any of the wrongs you committed in this lifetime. Your loved ones will be waiting for you."

She swallows hard, and I get the feeling there are quite a few wrongs she has to atone for.

"Your help today was very much appreciated, and I'll be sure my guardian angel puts in a good word for you." *Right, Persephone?*

At that moment, the guardian angel in question pops in. "Don't go making promises you can't keep," she warns.

"Everyone deserves a second chance," I say as much to her as to Edith.

The ghost's head swivels to the right. "I see it. There's a doorway." Her hand goes to her chest. "The light is so beautiful. And Daddy. He's there."

I mouth a silent *thank you* to Persephone. "Of course he is," I tell Edith. "He's missed you every day, too."

"I'm coming," she calls to him before she points to the scattered remains of the boxes. "You'll make sure my possessions are properly taken care of, right?"

A drop of rain hits my cheek. I gesture at Sage and Kit. "The three of us will find good homes for all of it, I promise."

My friends nod. Edith frowns down at the waking Elias. He rolls his lower jaw around and tries to sit up. Logan is immediately there, grabbing him by the back of his hoodie and pinning him against his truck.

Edith begins to float away. "Tell him that I did love him, and I'll be waiting for him when it's his turn to move on."

I watch her smile and embrace her father before the two of them, along with the light, fade.

"She's gone," I tell the others. I walk over to Elias. "She wants you to know that she loves you and will be waiting for you on the other side."

He emits a great wracking sob and hangs his head.

"Jones is on his way," Logan informs me. "He said not to do anything until he gets here."

Fat raindrops begin to fall. "What should we do about this mess?" I ask. "It's going to get soaked if we don't gather it up and fast."

Logan uses his phone to snap a few photos and then a video as the storm begins to kick up. "Let's load the intact boxes into Sadie's van. I'll give Jones a record of the scene, and if he doesn't like it, he can take it up with me."

From a former football star to a successful lawyer, my husband is one of a kind. I set the crystal ball and fragment next to Tabby on the lawn, and my friends and I go to work to save what's left of Edith's belongings from getting drenched.

Unfortunately, we don't fare as well. The rain becomes a forceful drizzle, and Sage gently scoops up Tabby to take her home.

Kit retrieves the crystal ball and its broken piece. "This is all my fault, and I feel like I should fix it. If," she adds, "you trust me with it."

I give her an awkward hug around the giant sphere, blinking through the water running in my eyes. "You know I do. What happened here"—I wave a hand at Elias—"is not your fault. It's his."

She, too, trails off, taking Aunt Willa's crystal ball with her. I know it couldn't be in better hands.

"You better get back to the school," Logan says. "The concert should be over by now, but I bet they're still breaking down the stage. They could probably use your help."

I pull out my phone and text Lia. She assures me everything is under control. I cross my arms, plant my feet, and stare at the grieving Elias. A part of me feels sorry for him, but the rest of me is angry. "I'm not going anywhere until I get an apology."

The man's head snaps up, his eyes red. "You're not getting one."

That part of me that felt sorry for him evaporates.

Persephone, who is typically invisible to everyone but me, works her magic and appears right in front of him in physical form. "Give her the apology. It's the least you can do."

"She's right, you know," I say to him. I again wipe the rain from my eyes. "Grief can make us crazy, but stealing and hurting people is never the answer."

He chokes out a sob, the sound lost in the storm. "You don't understand. I'm nothing without her. My life meant nothing until I met her. That day, everything changed for me. Now she's gone, and I have nothing. *Nothing.*"

Once again, my heart hurts for him. It doesn't excuse his actions, but I know how awful it feels to lose a person you love. I take Logan's hand and squeeze it. "That kind of love is special, and you should honor it. Not by stealing her things from her granddaughter, though."

"Then how?" he asks.

"Go to Hawaii. Take the snow globe. Create a shrine to her with the keepsakes in that box she made for you."

He frowns, shakes his head, then seems to reconsider. "Do you think she'd like that?"

"Edith Haversham, being the center of your loving attention and getting a shrine because of it? I can't imagine anything she'd love more." As if some higher power agrees, the rain slows, and the wind dies.

Elias hesitates, but I see a spark of hope replacing the grief in his eyes. "She did love being the center of attention."

Jones arrives in his police cruiser. It may be a while before Elias has the chance to take that trip, but I decide to do whatever I can to lighten his sentence.

As if reading my mind, Persephone gives me a satisfied arch of her brows. Sherlock appears and winks. They vanish together as Jones exits his vehicle.

Logan pulls me close and kisses my temple. "Good job. I'm proud of you."

"Me?" I pull away enough to look at him. "Why?"

"You help people, no matter what. Takes a big heart to do that, especially when you're scared."

"Don't let me interrupt," Jones says, stepping onto the sidewalk, "but can we get back to what happened here?"

Logan and I grin at each other. "Elias has agreed to return all the stolen items," I tell the detective, "and he wants to make it up to Sadie and the others, don't you, Elias? He has a date with Hawaii in his future, and he'll do whatever is necessary to keep that engagement."

Jones gives me a questioning look. "And the crystal ball?"

"Returned. No reason to press charges on my account."

He glances at Logan, scrutinizing a bruise and a shallow cut on my husband's face. "And you? Let me guess, you're not pressing charges either?"

I squeeze Logan's hand. He gets the message and gives Jones a shrug. "For what?" He levels Elias with a hard look, warning him that he better never try anything like this again. "We had a talk, is all."

"Sure you did." The detective grabs Elias and herds him toward the rear passenger door. "I'll be in touch for the full account next week."

Sadie arrives, her eyes rounding at the sight of the broken items. "What did you do to my stuff?"

Jones drives away, and Elias peers out the back at us. I point at him. "He'll be returning the stolen items, but a few of the things you were going to take to the Goodwill didn't survive the storm."

She gives me a confused look, and I change the subject to tell her that her grandmother has passed over. I mention the box she packed for Elias and the fact they really did love each other.

At first, she seems to disregard his depth of grief, but as I relay his exact words, she swoons a little. "Aww, that's sweet. And Nana loved him more than she did most any of us, I guess. I hope I find someone like that to spend my life with."

We talk a bit more and then say goodbye.

The stage is down, Lia is checking items off my list on the clipboard, and Daddy and Mama invite us over for dinner.

"After I clean up," I tell them, soaked to the bone but happy.

NINETEEN

The following two weeks are relatively uneventful. The summer wedding season kicks into high gear, and Rosie, Jenn, and I are swamped with routine, day-to-day jobs. We successfully marry off three couples and orchestrate a family reunion, a fortieth birthday party, and an adoption celebration.

The *Tribune* runs a glowing article about the success of the market. One paragraph mentions the stolen items but commends the police department's quick and effective action in bringing the culprit to justice. I struggle not to roll my eyes when Logan reads that to me.

I call a post-market Chamber meeting to discuss what worked and what we can improve for the next one. Delegating is a challenge for me since I'm a wee bit of a control nut. I do my best, however, and designate three committees—one to handle the farmers, crafters, and service providers, another for the flea market sellers, and a third to coordinate the food trucks and performers.

Lia attends with Wrenlee and Travis, volunteering them to head up each one. Outside of me and Baylor, the members have misgivings about our teenage friends' abilities.

Lia makes a convincing case when she presents a Power-Point presentation and hands out impressive resumes for herself and her friends. The board meets them halfway, matching each of them with an adult to co-lead the committees. Wrenlee and Baylor will coordinate the flea market sellers. Travis and Brax will handle the food trucks and performers. Lia and I are the final team, organizing the rest.

Sadie convinces Carl Anderson and Lorna Cummings not to press charges. The necklace and puzzle box are found among Elias' things, and Jones holds them as evidence—but Sadie calls to tell me she found them on the back porch, along with the orange cat who was hanging around the market. My grandmother—at work again.

While Jones charges Elias with theft, creating a disturbance, and a few other misdemeanors, he's released on probation, requiring him to seek grief counseling and perform twenty hours of community service.

I'm surprised when he shows up on my doorstep as part of his sentence.

"You saved my life," he says. "I owe you. I'm here to assist the Chamber or the library or...whatever...with any project you deem appropriate."

I'm stunned into silence for a moment, but thankfully, I have enough of Mama's brains and ingenuity to come up with something on the spot. "How are you at building things?" I ask.

He shrugs. "All right, I guess."

"Baylor needs new shelving units for the children's

fantasy and history sections at the library. She's been obsessed with Pinterest boards and has sketched some pretty grandiose designs for them. She wants to spark the kids' imaginations and bring fantasy and history to life."

A faint smile graces his face, and I see a much younger man in it. "When do you want me to start?"

"Is this afternoon too soon?"

He's wearing his black hat, and he tips it at me. "I'll be there at one. Does that work?"

"I'll let her know."

He removes the hat and holds it over his heart. "I also came to give you that apology. I'm sorry."

I pat his arm. "Apology accepted."

"I know that crystal ball had emotional value to it, and I can't replace that, but I'll make it up to you somehow."

I glance toward my office, where the repaired ball sits on a wooden holder. "I appreciate the offer, but it's not necessary. We're good."

I see him off and return to work. Persephone has left me alone during this grace period, and I'm grateful. Crossing two ghosts on top of everything else seems to have put me in good standing with her. I'm sure it won't last, but I'm so busy, I don't worry about it.

June is approaching, and so is my first anniversary with Logan. We were officially married in the backyard a year ago. As I gaze out the kitchen window a few hours later, watching my grandmother in human form and my grandfather in his ghostly one down by the creek laughing and teasing each other, I think about holding a small celebration to honor it.

It will be challenging to fit it in among our bridal events, but this is what I do—I help people celebrate the special moments in their lives. If I can't do that for myself, what's the point?

I'm still stewing it over, wanting to bring it up to Logan and get his opinion while we wash our dishes after dinner. The doorbell rings, interrupting my thoughts.

Tessy and Pete are grinning ear to ear when I open up.

"Sorry to drop in like this," Tessy says. "We wanted you to be the first to know."

Pete holds up a finger. "Technically, you're the second. We had to tell the girls first."

I don't need to see the pretty ring on Tessy's finger to know what they're about to tell me. "Why don't you come in?"

She grabs his hand. "We don't want to intrude. We just wanted you to know that we're getting married."

"That's wonderful. I'm so happy for you."

"I want your next available appointment to discuss the wedding and reception," she says.

"I'll check my calendar and text you tonight."

She throws her arms around his neck. "See? I knew she'd do it."

He winks at me over her shoulder. "Thanks, Ava."

I know his gratitude is for more than making his bride happy. "You're very welcome."

They leave, and I find Logan in our favorite spot in front of the fireplace. It's too warm for a fire, but we still share a glass of wine, the cats and dog joining us.

"I know you still have concerns about everyone's safety," he tells me, his thumb tracing circles on the back of my neck, "but I believe the rewards are far greater than the risks."

I clink my glass to his and take a sip. "You're right."

He stops massaging my neck and puts a hand to his ear. "What was that? It sounded like you said I'm right."

I playfully punch him, and he laughs. "If only they were all as easy as Olivia."

"Do you think she'll show up at Pete and Tessy's wedding?"

I shrug. "She gave him her blessing. I'm sure she'll be looking out for him and the girls as long as they live."

I stroke both cats, enjoying their purrs as they slowly sink into sleep. Moxley lays at our feet, also drifting off. Things turned out better than I expected, and I'm pleased.

Tabby strolls in, flicking her tail and heading for the stairs. She's fully recovered and peers at me between the spindles as she climbs.

"Where's she going?" Logan asks.

Persephone is next to materialize, motioning for me to follow. "We have a problem."

Doing my best imitation of a combination of Mama and Lia, I sigh dramatically and tip my head back. "What now?"

Logan lifts his brows in question. I point to my grand-mother's vanishing form, tail still flicking. "It seems I'm wanted upstairs."

"Should I come with you?"

I pat his leg and set my glass on the coffee table. "I'll call if I need you."

Following them, I climb to the second floor and look up when Persephone points at the attic steps. "What is it?" I ask.

"I've just been made aware of a situation that we need to handle," she says, without a lick of sarcasm or pushiness in her voice.

If anything, her lack of emotion makes me wary. "A situation in my attic?"

I find myself following her and the cat into the dark, dusty third floor. Night has fallen, and I flip on the single light that hangs from the rafters. It throws layers of shadows over the collection of furniture, trunks, and discarded boxes of belongings that I've never found time to sort through.

Tabby hops over stacks of books, magazines, and newspapers, then weaves behind a dress form and wooden rocking chair. She perches on top of a chest with metal hinges and leather buckles.

Persephone juts her chin. "Open it."

It's not as easy for me to get to it as it was for the cat. "I could use a flashlight."

"You won't need it in a minute," my guardian angel says.

A chill slides over my shoulder. "Just tell me what's inside that's so important."

She shakes her head. "This is one of those times when I can't say anything. All I can do is point you in the right direction."

The chill curls around my spine. I have to move the dress form out of the way and I sneeze from the dust from the newspaper stacks as I relocate them as well. I finally make it to the chest, and Tabby jumps down.

"I'm not going to like this, am I?"

Neither of them replies, and I reach for any kind of psychic message that might come through to warn me before I lift the lid. I'm not like Kit, Sage, or my aunt. There's a lot going on inside my brain, and I am imagining a whole lot of unnerving things that could be inside.

Best to get it over with.

The leather straps are worn and closed like a belt buckle. I wrestle with the tight material to release the clasp, then brush the dust from my hands. "Okay," I say, dragging up as much courage as I can. "Let's see what secrets you're hiding."

Of all the things I thought my aunt might have stored in this chest, what I see is not one of them.

At first, I think my eyes are deceiving me. Or that maybe it's a Halloween prop.

The smell that emanates from the chest tells me differently. I cover my nose and mouth with a hand, partly to shut out the odor and partly to hold in my cry of disbelief. My shadow falls over the contents, and I shift, trying to get more illumination on them. Unfortunately, that doesn't help.

It's no prop.

What I'm looking at inside Aunt Willa's trunk is a...

"This has to be a trick," I say. "A mistake."

"It's not," Persephone argues. "A scandal, yes. You have quite a mystery to figure out, Ava, and it looks like your aunt has something to answer for."

Blank, bottomless eye sockets stare back at me. Below them, a set of teeth seem to grimace.

This is so much worse than anything I'd imagined.

Locked away in this abandoned trunk in my attic is a human skeleton.

DON'T MISS *Skeletons and Scandals, Confessions of a Closet Medium, Book 10*, releasing in 2025!

VISIT MY STORE

Did you know you can buy directly from me? When you do, the retailer doesn't take a cut and I can pass on the savings to YOU!

https://www.nyxhalliwell.com/books

Benefits:
 You can find ALL my books in one place
 SAVE money
 EARLY access to new releases
 Special Collections and Limited Editions
 Support a small business

Why Buy Direct?
 When you purchase a book by your favorite author, electronic or print, on retailer platforms, the company keeps 30-70% of the sale, leaving the author with little to no profit (after the company deducts delivery fees, taxes, and other fees).

Buying directly from the author means that more goes to them so they can keep turning out stories for you. Every published story, every book, requires cover art, editing, and hours and hours of the author's time simply to create it. Not to mention overhead costs, such as websites, newsletters, writing software, graphics programs, advertising, taxes, etc.

In addition, one of the big-name retailers requires exclusivity, and all of them have terms of service and rules and regulations that make it challenging and time-consuming for an indie author to navigate the publishing world.

Most of us would MUCH rather spend our time creating more stories for YOU, rather than trying to jump through the hoops at the retailers. Buying direct from your favorite authors (where available) helps ensure that an author you love is not subject to unexplained account closures, withholding of royalties, censorship, and other issues that can affect their livelihood.

I've experienced ALL of these. By buying direct, you help put control of my work back in my hands - and I can continue to write more.

Either way, thank you for supporting me! I understand buying direct doesn't work for everyone and even if you use the retailers to buy my books, I appreciate you!

Happy reading,

Nyx

https://www.nyxhalliwell.com/books

YOU'RE INVITED!

Do you have a passion for my stories?

Want more from my characters?

How about early access to ALL my new releases?

My reader community is for YOU!

Try my **VIP reader community!** You'll get all these perks:

Writing Updates so you know what's in the works and how soon you can get it

Special Content, including recipes, puzzles, coloring pages, and more

Early Access to new stories

Pics of my pets (all are rescues and they "help" me write and edit) and my crazy plant collection

You're invited! What are you waiting for?

I'm in! Give me more stories!

READY FOR MORE MAGICK?

Don't miss the next exciting adventure! Sign up for Nyx's Cozy Clues Mystery Newsletter.

And check out these magical stories:

Sister Witches Of Raven Falls Mystery Series
Sister Witches of Raven Falls Special Collection
Of Potions and Portents
Of Curses and Charms
Of Stars and Spells
Of Spirits and Superstition
Sister Witches of Raven Falls Special Collection

Confessions of a Closet Medium Cozy Mystery Series
Confessions of a Closet Medium Special Collection
Pumpkins & Poltergeists
Magic & Mistletoe

Hearts & Haunts
Vows & Vengeance
Cupcakes & Corpses
Tea Leaves & Troubled Spirits
Haunted Honeymoon
Wedding Bells & Psychic Spells
Phantoms Are Forever

Confessions of a Closet Medium Cozy Mystery Series

Sister Witches of Story Cove (Formerly Once Upon a Witch) Cozy Mystery Series

Cinder
Belle
Snow
Ruby
Zelle

Sister Witches of Story Cove Complete Set

Witchy Candy Shop Mysteries

Tricks and Treats
Candy and Creeps
Gum and Ghouls (releasing 2025)

MEET NYX

USA Today bestselling author Nyx Halliwell loves writing magical stories as much as she loves baking and crafting. She believes cats really can talk (please don't tell her three rescue puppies), and yes, she sees ghosts.

She enjoys binge-watching mystery and paranormal shows with her hubby and reading all types of stories involving magic. She talks to trees, has too many crystals, and drinks far too much tea.

Check out her online store and sign up for her Cozy Corner newsletter at https://www.nyxhalliwell.com.

DEAR MAGICAL READER

Thank you for reading this story! It is an honor and a privilege to write books for you. I'm an indie author and every fan is important to me. I pour my heart into each story and do my best to bring you a delightful escape from the real world.

R eaders are the key to my success - not a traditional publishing deal (had four), an agent (had two), or a publicity team (yep, you guessed it, had several of those as well.)

Those of you who read my books and love my characters and worlds, and who then tell others, are like the best of friends. I adore you and will keep writing if you keep reading!

If you'd like to learn about my other books, sales, and special promotions, please sign up for my newsletter at https://www.nyxhalliwell.com.

Support me directly (no retailer taking their cut), grab special edition box sets, and get new releases before they are

out at retailers by visiting my store https://www.nyxhalli
well.com/books. I have sales and offer NEW RELEASES
early! Check it out.

Last but not least, if you enjoy grittier, but still fun,
urban fantasy, paranormal romance, or romantic suspense,
visit my pen name http://www.mistyevansbooks.com to see
those books.

Thank you for supporting my dream.

Blessed be,

Nyx 🤍